# HOW TO LOSE A HUSBAND

ANTONIA 'TOYA' WRIGHT

WITH CARLA DUPONT HUGER

*Toya xo 2018*

Copyright © 2016 by Toya Wright Publishing
ISBN: 978-0-9972178-0-3

Credits
Editorial: Dr. Erica Mills
Cover Shot: DeWayne Rogers
Cover Design: Howard Ross

# DEDICATION

First and foremost, I would like to thank God for the many blessings. I would like to thank my husband, Mickey Wright; my parents Anita Johnson and Walter Andrews; my beautiful daughter Reginae Carter; my lifelong friend Dwayne Carter; my siblings; my best friends Danielle Johnson, Lidia Muse, and Ashley Darby for showing me that real friendships still exist. My mentor/auntie Kristalyn Holden for all of the great advice she's given me over the years. My manager Rick George, my attorney Alcide Honore and last but not least #TeamToya and everyone who has supported me over the years...family, friends and fans. I love y'all. I hope you guys enjoy my new book *How to Lose A Husband*.

~ *Toya Wright* ~

# HOW TO
# LOSE A
# HUSBAND

# CONTENTS

# INTRODUCTION

*I'm* Lola, the one giving up the juice. You are about to be entertained by a few stories about me and my girls. These are my divas, my bitches, my ride-or-dies. These girls hold me down, wipe my tears and give me advice. I know you have your own group of divas, too. No matter what, we got each other's back...always.

Just like any other clique, we go through some shit. We put our hearts out there, we talk shit to each other, gang up on the world and raise our children. We get money while managing to hold our heads up in the face of adversity. We're good, as long as we got each other.

My life is probably the most normal. I have a husband of 15 years and identical twin boys who are 14, yeah, we got pregnant quick! I work as an accountant and my wonderful husband is a doctor. That's it. My Divas? I live vicariously through them. I see what they see, know what they know and hurt when they hurt.

They give me all the tea. I hear it from all of them and sometimes from the streets, too. Listening to the latest bit of drama one day, I thought, *Damn somebody should make a movie outta this!* So here you go, all for your reading pleasure.


*Didididididididi! Didididididididi!* British's head lifted off of her satin pillow case ever so gently. It was purple to compliment the gray, purple and white décor scheme in her room. There were hints of silver, too.

*Didididididididi! Didididididididi!* Waking up to her alarm clock every single day was something she was trying to get used to, but she knew exactly where it was located. Her arm flung wildly over to the nightstand. Without even turning her head toward the discounted Rooms To Go furniture next to her bed, British slapped the alarm clock into snooze.

She knew what time it was, but that didn't phase her one bit! She nestled back into the dreamy pillow top mattress, pulling the fluffy duvet back to envelope her. Between the eye mask she wore and the sanctuary of a bed she slept in, it often took an act of God to move her out of bed every morning. Eventually, she'd make it to the desk in her home office, then on to the spare bedroom that served as her workroom. She recently started setting her alarm to increase her productivity during the day. The next ten minutes were crucial. And maybe even the next ten after that, if she tapped the snooze button again. She readjusted herself in the bed, attempting to get another few sweet moments of shut eye.

All of a sudden, her eyes bolted open. *Stacks told me he was going to call me back*, she thought fumbling for her phone. She located it snuggled amongst the sheets and conjured up enough strength to turnover. Laying on her side, she swiped to the right and entered her four digit passcode. No new calls, no text messages. British was pissed! She rolled her eyes and said, "I know how to find out where this muthafucka went last night," in a groggy voice.

British found the Instagram icon on the bottom right of her screen and hit it while she simultaneously repositioned herself on pillows. The little circle at the top of the screen was going around and around, but her screen was blank.

"Come on, shit!" she croaked, impatiently growing upset anticipating that Stacks had let her down again. She double clicked the bottom of her phone, swiped the Instagram app up to close it, then pressed it on the home screen again.

"Bingo," a popular gossip column maintained one of the most widely recognized pages on Instagram. She followed a handful of them, which is how she kept up with celebrities and wannabe celebrities. CelebMail bragged about having close to two million followers. It was a trashy site that posted any and everything. Half of the stories could not even be validated, but they made for juicy gossip.

*Stacks Pays Bills At The G-Spot Strip Club in Atlanta*, the caption read. It was a picture of Stacks sitting down holding a brick of money with a stripper standing on stage in a mountain of cash. British grunted, she was hot. "So you spending money on these hoes, but you can't spend on me? Then you got the nerve not to even call me?"

*Dididididididi! Dididididididi!* British's ten minute snooze time was up. She tossed the phone on the bed pushing the covers back. She drug herself into the bathroom, back tracked a few steps to grab the phone off of the comforter, then scurried into the bathroom to handle her business.

By lunchtime, British had still not heard anything from Stacks. She already knew it was because he had been drinking. That was his lifestyle, though. He was a prominent rapper on the scene. He had been nominated for Grammys long before she ever met him. As an industry fave, if he graced a track it was guaranteed to be hot. He never missed. Stacks' first album went triple platinum back when people actually spent money buying albums. Fans couldn't wait for his sophomore effort, while critics were anticipating a total failure.

Without apology, his second album crushed the charts. In popular cities with multiple urban radio stations, his songs could be heard on all of them simultaneously. Every hour on the hour, Stacks was getting paid. In his home city of Atlanta, love was never lost. The more his fame grew abroad, the more his city embraced him. Keeping with the gritty nature of his rhymes, he had to maintain appearances in the places and doing the things he talked about. It also kept him close to his people, the fans.

His stripper anthem, "Private Dance For Me" was the top single on the charts in 2010. He introduced it in the strip club and filmed the video there as well. The Atlanta culture almost deemed it an absolute must to introduce a song in the strip club. If the strippers liked it, you had a hit.

When British met him, she knew what time it was. There was no doubt that he would be in and out of strip clubs, making club appearances on the regular and hopping on last minute flights at any time of day…or night. She was probably more jealous that she wasn't with him, raining dollars and smacking butt naked ass, than she was that he hadn't called her. She felt entitled to be his girl.

All The Divas knew the truth. Stacks belonged to somebody else. There was no mistaking who he was with. Stacks was a married man with two kids. His wife wore a fat-ass, 10-carat sparkler, according to the blogs. They had been together for years.

As far as British was concerned, she played her role well. He took her around with him. Her Divas and his boys knew what time it was, but nobody else did. She was aware of her reputation for having her legs open, so when paparazzi came around, she slid out of the frame or turned her back. So she couldn't understand why Stacks didn't call her to go to The G-Spot. By the end of the day, she gave in and called him. No answer.

The Divas found their way to happy hour. As you can imagine, British got there first. I pulled in second, we walked in and told them to give us a table in the back. We had to do that anytime Kennedi or Sade came out with us.

Once we were seated, I bee-lined to the bathroom to wash my hands. I'm kind of a germophobe. As soon as I got back to the table, British started going in.

"Man, I am so through with Stacks!"

"No, you're not," I brushed her off laughing.

"I am…not, through, like all the way…but like, you know?"

"Mmmm, nope! I sure don't."

"I mean, he tried it."

"Why? It's nothing he ain't done before."

"I know, but like…enough is enough."

"Enough is enough of what?" Kennedi jumped right on in, having found her way to the back of the restaurant. She flashed her honest smile and tilted her head. Her hair was still in a ponytail from her workout. She practically lived in workout clothes, so that was nothing new.

"Stacks! I'm done with him."

"Oh girl," Kennedi reached for the drink menu, knowing good and well she wasn't going to drink.

"He went to the G-Spot last night. I was not invited, he didn't tell me what he was doing and he hasn't called me all day!"

"That man doesn't owe you anything," Kennedi said. She slid the drink menu back in its place.

"Did it ever occur to you, Ms. British...that he was with his lady? His wife?" I chimed in. Sometimes it was necessary to remind her that Stacks was not her man. On the other hand, she was his piece. British had pretty much cut all of her dudes off for him back when he told her he wasn't caking her for the next nigga.

"He can't love her," she defended.

"It doesn't matter. They have two kids together. And years between them! He's not leaving her, British."

British just looked down at the table. I guess I took some of the wind out of her sails. It was always messed up that she dealt with a man who was already in a relationship, then for her to actually think she could break up his home was just taking it to a whole 'nother level.

British's M.O. was to mess with guys who were spoken for. It came honest to her. Her mother was the same way. Her mom *stayed* in some other woman's bed. That was the environment British grew up in. She heard her mother talking to her friends about her conquests, where being a side chick was glorified.

Now, British was at a point where she was ready to settle down and be a girlfriend, a real girlfriend. All of her friends were married, had been down the aisle at least once, or were getting there. They were having families and enjoying doing couple shit. Instead, British realized Stacks was the biggest baller she had ever landed and if he left his girl, it needed to be for her. Now, she was stuck trolling Instagram and gossip blogs for the latest on him.

But when they were together, their pillow talk used to be so sweet. He was going to take care of her, claim her in public; she would never have to worry about being secure again. They would have their own kids and raise them together. His actions though, they were another beast. He was seen taking his wife on shopping sprees and sometimes documenting it himself on his own Instagram and Twitter. His wife was laced with the best! Always fly! They had houses on two coasts and one in between, and are always seen wearing custom designer gear and diamonds. That damn girl was dripping in diamonds! A trip to the top jewelers in New York, L.A. and Atlanta seemed like an everyday affair, they even loaned her jewels to wear. It just left British stewing mad. And hurt.

"Why do you do that?" British asked me.

"Because I'm your friend. You're working yourself up for no reason. What? Am I supposed to just cosign with you because you're my girl? Hell no! You are wrong, British. You are screwing someone else's man. You should not want to be a side chick; you should want someone to stand before God and marry you. But, if you must settle for being a side chick, then be a side chick and shut the hell up. The decisions he makes do not really affect you."

"Hola chicas!" Madison piped up. She greeted us all with this weird cheek-to-cheek thing she does. She puts her cheek to yours, then closes her lips and blows air to make it bubble out.

"Looks like I walked up on some tea," she carefully placed her suit jacket on the back of the chair.

"Chile, just British and Lola with their usual Stacks banter," Kennedi volunteered.

"Kill it! I don't want to hear about his lame ass. What's next on the table for discussion?"

The mood was still a little tense; the waitress came over at the right time. As she took our drink orders, two ladies came up to the table. I already knew what they wanted, we all did. Kennedi smiled and started rubbing her tongue over her teeth to make sure there was no lipstick on them.

"Kennedi! We don't want to bother you," one of the girls started.

"It's fine ladies! How are you today?" My girl was happy, basking in the recognition. She made her way into a standing position.

"Can we please take a picture with you?"

"This is my fabulous side," Kennedi teased and flashed her pearly whites. Her soon-to-be-ex-husband spent a grip on that five digit smile. Her teeth were perfect and the brightest white possible. The fans breathed an obvious sigh of relief.

"I'll take it," I volunteered because it was obvious they both wanted to be in it.

They thanked me profusely and Kennedi told them to @ her in their post on social media and they went back to their table.

"That shit never gets old!" Kennedi said beaming. Unlike some stars who shy away from attention, she did not mind the picture and autograph circus that came with stardom. At least she knew she was still somewhat relevant.

"Can we take a picture with you?" British mocked the fans and we all laughed. The drinks came and we enjoyed a little girl time.

"Madison, how was work, Boo?"

"Winning cases as u-zhu-while," Madison smacked her lips.

"This year started off so fucking crazy! All of us are going through something," British said.

"Except Lola's ass," Madison joked. "Lola never goes through anything!"

"That's why we all call her!" Kennedi squealed giving Madison a high five. They missed British's side eye.

"This Paris shit is the icing on the cake! I needs me a getaway," British said.

"Let's do it."

"Girls' trip!"

"Girls' trip!"

"I'm tired of talking about it, y'all." Kennedi said. "I can have this trip planned for us in a week. Let me know something for real!"

"Yaaaaaas, Kennedi! Use your name card, hunty!" British clapped. Madison immediately opened the calendar app on her phone.

"Mmmmm, I can sneak away from the 6th through the 14th. That's only three weeks away, so y'all better figure something out. After that, I have a huge murder trial to prepare for."

"I can slide the 9th through the 14th," I let them know. "Paris needs to relax, relate and release."

"I'm free for life!" British blasted.

"Divas," Kennedi held up her glass, "here's to finding somebody's beach…"

"…to fuck up!" British jumped in. "It's going to be so dope. We can shop and swim and drink and party. And the men, Lord, the men!"

"British, we know you'll find a party and a man," I added. She just lifted up her eyebrows and gave me duck lips. I didn't care about her little play-play attitude. This trip was going to be awesome. I was sure we would end up on an island in the

Caribbean somewhere. I couldn't wait to be touring the Caribbean with my BFF's without a care in the world. I had to make sure to leave all my baggage stateside and encourage them to do the same.

# BRITISH

*We* arrived on the beautiful, sunny isle of Tortola. Words almost cannot even describe how beautiful this place was. Even from the tarmac, we could see God's hand in the place. It very possibly could have been the feeling of leaving behind worries, angst and stress back in The States. I know for me, it was such a relief to be getting away. That was the reason for the whole girls' trip, to kind of help us unwind from the crazy shit going on in our lives. We all had so much going on, we didn't know which way was up.

The door to our private jet opened. Instantly, the smell of warm, salty air permeated the cabin. We all inhaled deeply and burst out laughing because the sound was so collective, it was apparent we all did it at the same time.

"Good afternoon, ladies!" An airport attendant announced once he reached the top of the stairs. His accent was hella exotic. He only stood partially inside, but we could hear him just fine. He was tall, nicely built and not bad on the eyes. Not gorgeous, but not bad.

"Afternoon," we replied.

"Welcome to the British Virgin Islands. The island you are on right now is the island of Tortola. We are working to get you off as soon as we can," he began looking around the plane at each one of us. "This is one of our busiest seasons and unfortunately, the wait right now is about an hour and...Kennedi?" He paused in mid-sentence. His gaze didn't even make it around to Sade.

"Yes," she said, smile beaming. She seductively batted her eyes.

"Hol' on," he said in that strong accent of his. He ran down the stairs and we couldn't see where he went.

"Leave it to this bitch to get us past some shit," British started up.

"Yup, you already know they are about to whisk us off this damn plane!" Paris added. We felt the vibrations of someone running up the stairs. Our gent was back.

"Right this way ladies, don't worry about 'cha bags. Just grab your purses, jackets and anything in the cabin you want to keep your hands on. Follow me." He stood at the foot of the stairs helping us down one by one. Sade was the last one off of the plane. He stopped breathing when he saw her.

They must have announced that Kennedi was on the plane inside of the tiny airport. I mean, it couldn't have had more than two or three gates, half of the building seemed to be glass and we could see people clamoring to catch a glimpse of who was coming in. There was a window wall separating the public side from the private side. People were shouting, clapping and snapping pics. Our star, Kennedi led the pack walking next to our gent.

"We love you here," he had to raise his voice to speak over the cheering. "Your songs were very popular, the radio still plays your hits," he told her. She liked to hear that all the years of hard work she put in was not lost and it still offered her perks of notoriety. She was not one of those stars who swept their past accolades under the rug. She appreciated each and every fan, every pic and every gesture.

"Thank you, sir. That really means a lot to me."

"This room is where we will process you through customs. We cannot have you in the general area for obvious reasons. Plus, we like to take care of our upper echelon guests. Sit back and relax for a moment. I will have someone come process you quickly. While you wait, let me offer you beverages. What will you have?"

"Do you have some of that Henny White?" I asked. He looked and gave me the 'I'm walking through church during service' finger telling me to hold on. He brought back an unopened bottle and poured us all shots and passed them out.

"This is to us ladies," I spoke. "We are here to enjoy ourselves, let loose and have some fun. No worries about what we left behind. Cheers to the islands!" It was going to be a good trip.

"Cheers!" We all downed our shots, except Kennedi.

"Why are you baby-sitting that shot, Kennedi?"

"C'mon Kennedi!" Sade urged halfheartedly. "We ain't gon' let you babysit drinks all week. You can forget that, chile."

"Kennedi, everybody else took their shot. Why are you just sitting there hanging on?" I continued.

"Y'all know I don't drink like that," Kennedi tried to get out of it.

"Take the damn shot," I said.

"But…"

"Take the damn shot!" We all yelled. She took it…finally.

"Damn! You are worse than my baby taking medicine!" Paris jumped in. We giggled, and sat down. By that point, another airport attendant came in to check us through customs. The process was quick, and then our gent appeared again.

"Ladies, I will walk ya to the curb. Sade Dorsett," he reached down and kissed her hand, "I love you." He wrapped her arm around his and walked us out. The taxis jetted us to the dock. We found our private yacht, boarded and began the trip out to the island where we were staying.

The captain had hip-hop music playing, which we could all vibe to. There was juice, alcohol, finger foods like crackers, fruit and cheese on the boat. It was so refreshing to be catered to. We paid to get that kind of service. We didn't want to worry about anything while we were there.

The view was absolutely breathtaking. The balmy wind coursed through my cornrows sitting on the back of the yacht. Some of the islands were inhabited and I could easily see the businesses and homes dotting the side, others were just gorgeous floating masses of green trees and rock. Oh, and the water! Lord Jesus, the water was so blue, it looked like you could see straight down to the bottom. The only times I have ever seen anything that remarkable was on advertisements to seduce you into visiting.

Everybody was talking about how striking the scenery was, what they wanted to eat and things they wanted to see. The Divas were taking pictures of each other and the view. Except British and Paris. Paris was at least half-ass trying to loosen up. British was in her own world. She was usually one of the more rowdy chicks in the bunch, it was odd to see her sitting there

so quiet. I knew what was on her mind. That damn
Stacks! Let me dive on into how that whole
catastrophe came to be.


British was introduced to Stacks through a
mutual friend, King. Well, friend is a bit of a strong
word. He was another fellow rapper who British used
to fuck. Stacks and King were really cool, they had
worked on a few projects together and partied together
through the years. King used to date one of British's
home girls, Zyla.

Now, Zyla was a cool chick. She wasn't messy,
didn't keep up a lot of drama. If she fucked with you,
she fucked with you. It was that simple. She fucked
with British. The two of them were known to frequent
clubs and parties together. They were too fine to pay
for their own drinks and they knew it. They dressed the
part to snag the ballers.

Neither of them was a stranger to dudes with
boat-loads of money and tons of influence. Even back
in high school, British was pulling the popular guys. I
remember seeing her walking through the halls like
you couldn't tell her nothing. The other girls hated on
her more than they hated on me because she was so on
point and she had a stank attitude about it. She was
about 5'6", a little taller than average, with a beautiful
face and a banging body. From head to toe, she was
the quintessential dime. She never had a hair out of

place, was on point with her make-up according to the latest trends and let's not even get to her threads.

Not a single girl had a thing on British! Fly was not the word. She made her own stuff, like literally, sewed her own pieces. In high school, being with the popular guys, she really wanted to set herself apart. She knew there were girls digging her boyfriends and she did not want to dress like them, shop where they shopped or have the same hairstyles. Coming up with unique hairstyles was a little harder to maneuver, but she knew her originality could easily be shown through what she wore.

Her mother taught her: to get the man, she had to look the part. That's what she did. She started dabbling in design, buying fabrics and using patterns. As she mastered it, she wore her pieces to school and gave me some to wear as well. That was the real test. Once she got approval from picky peers, British never looked back. She began designing and sewing pieces for other "it" girls at school, and around town word quickly spread that her clothes were the shit.

She used the money she made to buy the flyest fabrics, take sewing classes and get access to cool add-ons like buttons, feathers and sequins. British took her design craft seriously. When most of her peers were heading off to college or making babies, she was creating a name for herself. Whether it was a dope boy, a stripper or a school teacher, British didn't care who wanted what, as long as their money was green.

This was back in the late 90's, before the internet was a mainstay for social popularity or exposure for businesses. British had to be smart in how she went about drumming up business for herself. She went to salons, barber shops, clubs, strip clubs and skating rinks. You name it, if there was a crowd of people there, so was she.

"Ooh girl! I like your top. Where did you get that?" The girls would ask.

"Oh, this? Chile please, I made it." She would answer nonchalantly, because truthfully, she already knew what their reaction was going to be.

"You made it?"

"Yeah."

"Can you make me something?"

"Here is my card. Page me, I can hook you and your friends up!" Adding that bit about the friends was a sales tactic to get their friends calling too, bringing her more business. It worked. She got an apartment by 19. Atlanta royalty started reaching out to her. She made clothes for basketball players' girlfriends and wives, football players' ladies and people on the music scene. She bought a beater car and upgraded it three times before buying her first brand new Mercedes by 23.

It was easy to see that design was her passion. It was the only thing she cared about. Her career was so busy she didn't even bother trying to have a relationship. She had friends or buddies, a cutesy code name for the niggas who took priority in fucking time. Literally. Her buddies were the ones who got to see her before anybody else. They may have been in town for a few hours or a few days; some of them lived there...but they were all spoken for. Either way, she made these dudes priority.

Then there were the guys who were just around, who she thought were fine or looked like they had a nice, strong back to lay pipe. For British, it was a power thing. She loved seeing how her body could bring them such pleasure. The harder they came, the more she got off. If they passed out asleep, sucked their thumb or shed a tear, British's ego was totally gassed.

Having sex filled a void in her life. There was little emotional attachment. The sex was a genuine need to feel loved. It was also what she grew up seeing. Her mom kept a steady rotation of men running through the house. British's father had a wife, which her mother knew when they started dating, before she wound up getting pregnant. Not wanting to have an abortion, British was born, but it was just her and her mother. The father never bothered showing up, even to the hospital.

With no man in her life to show her how a woman should be treated, she looked to her mother to teach her what to expect. What she learned was: no love, no trust, no commitment and no expectations. She was just out for what she could get.

It was no military secret that British was DTF, down to fuck...anywhere, anytime, just about any baller. Her name was mud, well, maybe not that bad, but the guys knew she would make herself available to them. Call British at midnight, she's on the way. See British in the club? She would leave with ya. Text

British at 5 a.m., she would rush over to get your rocks off and make it home to catch the sunrise. And what did she have for it? Nothing. Absolutely, nothing.

In the beginning, they would take her on trips, buy her bags and shoes, but the more she hoed around, the fewer benefits she got. She had been passed around so much, everybody knew that she was community property. A beautiful, thick piece of community ass.

British convinced one of her ballers to invest in her clothing line. She had money saved for that purpose, but why use her hard earned money when niggas in her bed were making hundreds of thousands and millions of dollars? It made much more sense to use their money, especially with them just pissing it away in strip clubs and bars. So she did. By her mid-20's, British had Atlanta on lock! Going around to find business for herself was how she met Zyla.

Zyla was a beautiful girl with a sordid past, like British had and they bonded well. They both were out for what they could get from guys and joked about it. The hot nightlife scene is where British was introduced to Ecstasy, or X for short. She saw people sitting in corners, on the floor or just standing there twirling lights around and was freaked out. She was thinking that they were too old to be fascinated by a damn light. Zyla told her, they were 'tripping on X', which basically meant high on pills.

She decided, what the hell and popped some too. I personally have never popped X, nor would I want to, but to hear her describe it sounds like a cool experience. British said all of her senses were heightened, especially touch, she was super horny and her body yearned to feel sensation. Popping pills became a normal thing for her. It made the sex better. Whether she had a booty call lined up or not, you can bet by the end of the night, she was going home with somebody.

When Zyla popped X, she had her men lined up, too. Put liquor on top of the pills and she wasn't good for shit. There were times when British had to cancel her plans or take Zyla home because she was too far gone.

King, one of Zyla's dudes, had a VIP booth in the club one night and they were getting lit! Zyla had already told him she wanted to give him some, so he didn't mind getting her liquored up. Once she popped the pill, though, it was over. By the end of the night, King decided to take them both home with him. British was not as far gone as Zyla, but King could not have it on his conscience if something were to have happened to her. When they got to his crib, he carried Zyla in first and put her in his bed, then helped British out of the car that was parked in the garage.

"Wassup, King?" She stammered, not even able to stand up all the way. He put his arm around her and she squinted her eyes trying to focus.

"C'mon gul, get yo' ass out dis car." He pulled her to a standing position.

"Why don't you get in…and get this ass," she laughed.

"C'mon…you're fucked up."

"I know and I want some dick." She looked around, "I don't see any other men around here, do you?"

"You don't want it," he said. He stopped trying to pull her out of the car.

"Mmmmk! But what if I do?" she asked no longer squinting.

"British."

"King. I see how you look at me. You wanna know what this snatch feel like." She grabbed his crotch. He grunted and licked his lips. He had enough liquor in his system not to need much affection to get the party started. "Look at that, I didn't even have to do anything." She pushed him back from the car door and slid to the edge of the back seat.

As King stood there, she unbuttoned his pants, then pulled his penis out and massaged it with her hands. He was hard and ready to go. Neither one of them stopped for two seconds to think about Zyla in the house upstairs. She was knocked the fuck out as far as they were concerned.

British stood up out of the car, pulled her skirt up and bent over using the handle of the door on one side and the frame of the car on the other for a little support. Then she took his tool and rubbed it up and down along the crack of her ass. He couldn't take it! He bent her over more and slid it in. They had sex right there in the garage.

The next morning, Zyla woke up to King in the bed next to her. She was surprised to see British on the couch. Then again, she realized she did not have much of a recollection of the night before.

A few days later, British was shocked to see King calling her phone. He told her he needed to talk to her, she gave him the address and told him to swing by. She was nervous, thinking he had some kind of come to Jesus moment where he felt bad about what they had done and was going to tell Zyla. British opened the door, he stepped in and cupped her ass with both hands, then smiled as wide as the Nile is long.

"Boy, get off of me!" she pushed him back a step. He put his hands back on her ass and started kissing her neck. That was all she needed. This time, neither of them could blame any substance. There was no X, no liquor, no weed, just air between them. They messed around for a few months until Zyla popped up at British's apartment and saw King's car there.

Zyla dismissed both of them. She wanted nothing to do with either of them. British and King didn't really call it quits, they just fizzled out. By then, the damage was done. She had lost a friend. But when Stacks made his way to Atlanta and was looking for a wham-bam-thank-you-ma'am, King recommended British. She had her own money, her own place, she was not attached, the sex was good and she didn't walk around spreading her business. It was a good situation for Stacks. Besides, it was King's way to set her up with a nigga who was gonna break her off every now and then the way King knew he wouldn't.

Stacks was no unknown underground rapper. He was hot shit and everybody knew it. He was lacing

British with all kinds of shit. Of course she preferred to wear her own designs because she could make herself one-of-a-kind pieces that no one else would have. That did not mean she turned her nose up to the usual suspects...Prada, Gucci, Chanel. He would have her meet him places, hook her up, then leave. It was no biggie to either one of them.

The first time she saw his wife in real life was on a shopping trip. He told her to meet him at Tiffany, he was taking his wife to pick up a few things. He made it very clear to her that she was his side chick and she needed to play her role. He had no intention of leaving his wife.

"Act like you don't even know me. If you start popping off at the mouth, you'll never hear from me again. It's not like she's gonna believe you anyway, it's your word against mine. And bitches come up all the time talking about they fucked me and I ain't never seen them before. Just be there like seven, I'll make sure we are there around the same time. Start picking some shit out and let me come to you. Capeesh?"

"Alright," she smiled. It wasn't anything new, British messing with a guy who was already attached, that's how she preferred them. Now, Stacks expecting her to go to the same store where he was shopping with his lady was definitely something different. She was used to shopping *for* the main chick, being with a dude helping him pick a gift for his wife or girlfriend, then grabbing something for herself, but never a situation like this.

Stacks was going to be hard to miss, wearing the cliché 'I'm a rapper' dark shades inside a building, with humongous diamond studs and a big chain of some sort that was just too ridiculous to be around a normal person's neck. She arrived just shy of seven and when approached, told them she was just looking around. He walked in about ten minutes later with his wife in tow. They were immediately greeted by a visibly anxious manager at the door and whisked away to a private room. About five minutes later, Stacks came out alone.

"British," he said pointedly.

"Stacks," she responded in kind.

"What did you find?"

"You didn't give me a budget." A salesperson walked over to them. She appeared to be familiar with Stacks, they shook hands and she smiled.

"Tell me what you want," he said.

"That depends...five stacks, ten stacks...twenty," her voice trailed off. He took a sip of the champagne the manager had given him in the back room. Stacks looked at the salesperson.

"Ten, put it on my card, but give her the receipt," Stacks pointed to British. He turned to walk away, smacked her hard on the ass, then made his way back to the private room. Ten stacks is easy to blow in Tiffany, British was gone by the time Stacks and his wife left.

The gifts and money were to pay British for keeping things discreet and save that snappy nappy dugout for him. Stacks was well aware of her reputation, but was not going to be caking her for the next nigga. He wanted her all to himself.

As with any 'sexship', a pseudo relationship where you meet primarily for sex and little else, British started to grow feelings. In her haze, she convinced herself that Stacks actually cared for her. Or maybe, during pillow talk he told her he did. She went from, fucking this nigga, to spending time with my baby. All the while, he was still, very publicly with his wife. I guess, I should give you her name. Kenya, her name is Kenya.

Stacks and Kenya were straight. He kept taking her on the red carpet and she moved around the country with him, sometimes with the kids, others without. It was very clear that he was not going anywhere.

The first time British told Stacks she loved him was a momentous occasion in her mind. That was not a word she ever threw around, but it was the only way to describe how he made her feel. I think it was just because she didn't have any other dudes to kick it with. Stacks made it clear that he wanted her to himself and she obliged. With no one else occupying her time, her mind developed a dependence on him, an affection.

"I got you," that was his response. That's all. British did a good job of barely being seen, not heard and hardly remembered. After bringing her around Kenya a few more times and British maintaining her role, Stacks got real comfortable. The rubbers went away, he would spend the night, they started actually hanging together instead of just fucking and meeting up to shop or club. He started taking her with him to the strip club, like showing up with her, being with her and leaving with her. Like I said earlier, strip clubs are the foundation of the Atlanta music scene, but also a breeding ground for rumors because you never know who will be there.

Stacks was smart enough to know that people would see them together in the strip clubs and start rumors. Kenya would probably trip about it at first, but she'd ask him, not find any truth to it. After that, she'd be irritated that people kept talking about it. So if anyone saw them together after Kenya had heard the rumors, Stacks could easily say, people were keeping up the story. He was having his cake and sho' nuff eating it too.

British was caught up. She knew it, he knew and The Divas knew it, too. Her design business was falling behind and she was not out trying to get new clients or extend contracts like before. At some points she barely had money coming in. As long as she had her Stacks, she didn't seem to care about much else.

I tried to get her to see that while her career was falling through the cracks, he certainly was not losing any money spending time with her. She shouldn't either. She wasted her precious design time trolling through gossip websites to see how often Stacks' name came up and what people were saying. Not only was she reading the articles, she was reading the comments also. She never let him know she was stalking his every move. She also wanted to see what the fans thought about his wife. It cracked her up to see that some people were not fans of Kenya's.

Stacks called British from the studio. They were supposed to be going to dinner, but he needed to stop by his makeshift office, which was really another apartment he had in the city that his wife didn't know about, then he would be on his way. British decided she would meet him there. Even though she had a spare key, British had been *trained* not to stop by without asking. She had no reason to go by, he was rarely there anyway.

She got there before he did and walked right up to the door, turned the lock and went inside. There was nothing office about it, Stacks had the spot completely laid out. It was a wonder he was able to keep it from Kenya the whole time. His stuff was all over the place. She saw a Rolex with diamonds on the bezel and a huge wad of cash lying on the table. His platinum chain was hanging off of the end table by the couch where some random bitch was laying. His shoes...*SKURRRR*... British tapped the girl on the shoulder waking her up.

"Who are you?" British asked. The girl instantly looked annoyed.

"Who are you?" She asked with an attitude.

"Bitch, this *my* shit!" British lied and held up the keys. She felt entitled to anything that was his.

"Oh, shit!" The girl snatched up her phone and ran into the bathroom, barricading herself inside. British went crazy.

"Who the fuck are you, Bitch?" British beat on the door. "Who...*HIT*...the...*HIT*... fuck...*HIT*...are ...*HIT*...you...*HIT*? Come out! Don't be scared now! You weren't scared when you were sleeping on my man's couch! Come out!" Meanwhile, the girl was inside on the phone calling Stacks. When he didn't answer, she called his friend.

"Mane, this is Monique!" She screamed into the phone to one of Stacks's friends who was only a few minutes away. "You gotta come over here! This crazy bitch just walked in and she's going...SHIT!" British stabbed a knife through the door.

"BRANG YO' NAPPY HEADED ASS HERE NOW!"

By that time, Stacks was parking outside. When he saw British's car, he knew he was about to walk into some drama. The door to the apartment was wide open and he could hear British yelling from where he stood. His heart instantly dropped to the pit of his stomach as he ran inside.

"British, stop stabbing the door!"

"You don't have the right to say shit to me!"

"Put the knife down!"

"Who the fuck is this bitch, Stacks?"

"She's here for Mane!"

"Bullshit!" Mane and another friend, Pat ran into the opened apartment. British was still standing next to the locked bathroom door riddled with holes from the knife. Stacks was standing closer to the door in a fight or flight stance with his arms outstretched.

"Mane, tell British Monique is here for you!" Stacks coaxed. His homeboys knew British and what time it was.

"British, you are trippin' gul, Monique is one of my bitches!" Mane laughed. He tried to lighten the atmosphere.

"Bitches?" Monique yelled.

"SHUT UP!" everybody screamed in unison. Feeling bold knowing there were three men in the apartment who wouldn't let a fight break out, Monique opened the door. She strolled out and just stared at British.

"Yes, I am here for Stacks, what 'chu gon' do? You ain't even his wife?"

"Bring your ass over here, bitch. I'll show you what I'll do." The ladies ran at each other, Stacks cornered British to take her into the room so Monique could get her stuff and get out.

British was all upset after it happened. She got in the car and peaced out. She refused to answer his calls or texts for a few days. Then, one day he popped up over her house. When she looked through the peep hole to see who was ringing the door bell, she saw a huge brown box. Just like that, they were right back at it. Stacks had her pegged. All he had to do was leave her alone for a few days to let her cool down and show back up bearing gifts.

Each time she took him back, British was devaluing herself. Basically, he was buying her. She was too stupid or too gone to care. He told her he loved and missed her. It made her feel good until he said he wasn't leaving his wife. He let British know he was comfortable with their relationship the way it was. She knew he was married when they met and she decided to play this part. Anytime British brought up the topic of him possibly leaving Kenya, he laughed.

Months and months went by without event until British told him, "I'm pregnant."

"I bet you are," he leaned over to her and began kissing her neck. British had decided to tell him just as they were about to get busy. He teased her with kisses down between her breasts and back up on either side of her neck. He sucked on her nipples using his tongue to flick them until they got hard again. He positioned himself between her legs, placing his head at her belly button. His lips touched her ever so gently. Low... lower...even lower.

"I'm serious Stacks."

"How are you pregnant, huh?" he asked softly in between kisses. He was ready to get back down to business. The stench of sex still lingered in the air from the first round.

"What do you mean, how? We have sex don't we? We haven't used rubbers in years!"

"You said you were on birth control!" His tone changed when he saw the conversation was not a joke.

"I never said I was on birth control."

"My pull out game is strong. Whose baby is that?"

"Nigga! How the fuck is the first thing out of your mouth, whose baby is this? You know damn well whose baby this is...It's yours fool!"

"Nah, British!" He sat all the way up. She stared at him, her eyes burning a hole through his face. Even though she was butt naked, he looked past the thick hips and full breasts right into her eyes. They were having an old school staring contest. Who was going to blink first?

"What the fuck does *nah* mean?"

"You can't have it."

"Stacks!"

"No, man! I was with Kenya when we met, British. We have a family." The words hit her like a dagger in the heart.

"So you just throw her up in my fucking face? Is that what this is?"

"Ain't nobody throwing shit! You have to go get rid of it. It ain't even a baby yet."

"Oh, oh, oh," she laughed loudly, "you talk shit about cumming in me when you fuck me raw. Now that there is a baby in there, it's a problem? I thought you cared about me." He could see in that moment, she was vulnerable. If he spoke to her gently, he may just get his way.

"I do care about you, Baby. There is a lot of love between us. This just really complicates things."

"I love you, Stacks. This baby was conceived in love."

"We will have to figure out something."

"I am...well, I was ok with playing the backfield. This changes things. I want this child to have a relationship with you." Stacks sat all the way up on the bed, he knew where this conversation was headed. British wanted more than this sexship. She wanted a real relationship. There was just a teeny, tiny problem, he was already in one.

The Divas were not excited about where this was headed. They had seen and heard about this happening so many times before with different chicks along the way. British had never considered having a child before, well, she thought about it only enough to know motherhood was not on her list of things to do. She was far too busy doing her. With Stacks, it was something different. No other guys demanded her full attention. His taking the lead turned her on. To her it signified that he really wanted her. He was right, this baby was going to be a game changer.

British envisioned her future with Stacks, like a real future. She saw them being together as an official couple and raising their child. When she spoke about it, I would ask her, "What about his family?" She would shrug her shoulders and continue on. My girl showed no regard at all for the lady in his life or the children he was already raising. It's like she didn't care about them at all.

It made me sick to see her carrying on like that. Especially with me being a wife thinking some trick like her could be plotting to end my marriage. The picture perfect view she had envisioned for her life escalated from only wanting to snag a baller all the way to becoming his wife. Even if she had to push someone else out of the way to do it.

One morning, British woke up having excruciating pain. She had never felt pain like that before. Her immediate first thought was the pregnancy. *Was this normal? This couldn't be normal,* she thought. She needed to get to the hospital. She got up and waddled to the bathroom, in her heart she knew something wasn't right. Looking down at her legs, she saw blood and her stomach got upset.

"No! No!" she spoke out loud to nobody but herself. She cleaned herself up and went to the emergency room. On the way there, she called me crying. She was half whispering, half crying so the only thing I could make out was the name of the hospital. I was frantic, honestly her pregnancy wasn't even on my mind. She had recently told us, but when you can't see a pregger belly and it's only the beginning, a fetus is the last thing on your mind.

I found her quickly. The nurses and doctor did the normal song and dance around the E.R. Upon doing an exam, they saw that she had suffered a miscarriage. The tears began to roll. I could tell she was hurt and embarrassed. Since I was not Stacks' biggest fan, British probably regretted calling me. She turned her face away from me so I couldn't see her tears.

Girl, please! We were in a tiny hospital room! Of course I saw the tears. I couldn't express condolences for something I didn't support. I got her back home and had one of the other girls go get her car. I called in some take-out from Cheesecake Factory to lighten her mood.

Food was the last thing she wanted, but it was there if she got hungry. I hung out with her for a while, in silence. The TV was on, but I could see her mind was in a different place. She was thinking about the child that she lost. The shot at having a family that was now gone. She never really wanted children...until she was about to have one. That left a burning desire in her heart to have a child between Stacks and herself. She dismissed herself from the living room and called Stacks.

"I just got back from the hospital."

"What's wrong?" Stacks asked genuinely concerned. I *know* that fool had his fingers crossed that she was calling to say she had a miscarriage or an abortion.

"Our baby's gone." Silence. She could not tell if he was doing the running man, flipping cartwheels or unmoved. One thing she was sure of, was that he wasn't upset.

"I'm sorry, I know it's something you really wanted."

Emphasis was on 'you'. Yeah, it was easy to be sympathetic since the thorn had been removed from his side. His mind told him he had to be more careful, her mind was already thinking about getting pregnant again. This time, on purpose.

Even though only her Divas knew about the pregnancy, she still felt like a change of scenery would do her good. Truth was, she had only known she was pregnant for about a month. In those four weeks, she managed to conjure up a whole new fantasy life for herself.

She and Stacks had a number of heart-to-heart conversations about their relationship. During the healing process, she could not have sex, but he made sure to spend quality time with her. He told her that after she told him about the pregnancy, he was thinking things over and had toyed around with the idea of leaving Kenya to be with her, he just had not had the conversation with either of them yet.

British began doing research on natural ways to increase fertility, what types of foods to eat, different positions to have sex in and even buying an African fertility statue for her place. The crazy part was how excited she got when she talked about eating healthier, taking prenatal vitamins and exercising. She was going all out trying to get pregnant for a man who only mentioned he *may* leave his wife. Never once did he put actions behind those words.

The whole time, we were fussing at her trying to get her to understand that she deserved better. Stacks was going to drag her as long as she allowed him to. Why would he go anywhere else when she gave all the goods she had? He got sex anytime he even thought about it. She wasn't seeing anyone else, nor was she making a public fuss of their relationship. His pull out game was strong, according to him. And going forward, he would be more careful.

He just asked for time. Damn, how much time did he need? British had been a faithful side chick for going on four years. His words may have said, "I'm going to leave Kenya," but his actions showed differently. Her nose was so wide open, that she couldn't see his actions, because the words painted the picture she so desperately wanted to see.

With a system chock-full of natural foods to get herself knocked up, British wanted to get away with Stacks to get him relaxed enough for things to "just happen." He wasn't letting his guard down enough for her to move forward with this planned pregnancy...planned only in her head.

"I really don't want to be here. I want to get away for a few days."

"I'm going to Houston for a while. Why don't you come to my house out there?"

Over the next few days, Stacks bought her a first class ticket to Houston on his flight. British was overjoyed. He asked for a little time in getting his affairs in order financially to figure out what he could offer Kenya in the divorce. He wanted Kenya and his kids to be comfortable. British obliged and knew it was only a matter of time before Stacks was parading her around as his lady.

She made the house feel like a home. Being there was just the change she needed. It had been a while since she had visited Houston and playing house with Stacks was something she had only dreamt of. Whatever time she rolled out of bed, if he was home, she cooked breakfast. They could let their guards down and relax around each other. Her cooking for a dude wasn't strange, but cooking nude for her man, *her* man was new territory.

British could feel Stacks come into the kitchen as she stood at the stove, scrambling eggs. His presence was welcomed, although she wanted him to think she didn't sense him there. She never looked behind her, but she could feel him there. She began winding her hips and clapping her ass. She knew it was a sight to see. Her body was still amazing. *Wap! Wap! Wap!*

"So it *is* true!" British heard a female voice say. Then she heard someone running up...or down the stairs. She couldn't even turn around quick enough. *Wap! Wap! Wap!* British picked up the frying pan and threw the eggs in the direction of the female voice. In a split second, she saw Kenya holding a pink Hermes using it to go up-side her head.

British started stumbling backwards and Kenya was lunging forward. British was ducking the hits, but searching for some shit to throw. Something, anything. The damn kitchen was so big and clean, everything was out of reach. "They told me Stacks was out here held up with a bitch. I told them my man wouldn't do that to me! And it's you! I've seen you! What's your name, hoe? Brittany...Brandy...?"

British was in complete shock. She was not prepared for this. Who told Kenya they were out there? How did she get all the way to Houston without Stacks knowing? This time, the shoe was on the other foot. Instead of her claiming Stacks and being mad at some random chick, his wife was about to whoop her ass!

"Kenya!" Stacks shouted. Kenya threw the purse at Stacks and jumped on British punching her. British lost her footing and Kenya got in several quick jabs to the face before Stacks could get her off. British got some punches in too, but Kenya had the upper hand in the surprise attack.

"What the fuck is this, Stacks?" Kenya was breathing heavily.

"It's not what it looks like!"

"Yeah, I bet! Niggas always say that dumb shit! You got this fucking whore who pops up on the blogs with you dancing butt-ass-fucking-naked in my kitchen, cooking for your black ass! How is that not what it looks like?"

"Listen, Baby."

"Baby?" both Kenya and British replied in unison even though his comment was directed to Kenya.

"Yeah, bitch...he said Baby!" Kenya yelled. Even in a 10,000 square foot home, Stacks was sure her voice could be heard outside. The women lunged at each other again. Stacks knew British would listen, so he picked up Kenya and turned his back to British blocking the hits.

"Go upstairs, British!" He yelled, Kenya's arms were flailing in the air. "Kenya!" He shouted letting her go.

"Why...how...how could you do this to me? Seven years...two kids! Word on the street is you tip-toeing with this bitch and I'm denying everything. You got me out here looking like a damn fool! I'm telling people Stacks ain't doing shit! And yo' slimy ass is bold enough to have this bitch in my goddamn house? My house Stacks! Probably fucking her in my bed!

What the fuck is wrong with you?" She slapped him. Her face was wet from tears.

"Baby, I'm sorry, she just..." He reached out for her hand. British, now clothed. Stood at the top of the stairs where she could see, but not be seen. She didn't like what she saw. Here was the opportunity to get her man.

"Stacks...I guess you didn't tell her about the baby we just lost!"

"Baby?" Kenya said breathlessly. "There... there...there was a...a baby?"

"Kenya," Stacks looked so dejected.

"There is nothing you can say to me right now Stacks, nothing!" Kenya marched back into the kitchen and picked up a knife. She ran around the other side of the kitchen island into the living room and started going absolutely ballistic. British watched as Kenya sliced up the couch, threw vases and picture frames across the room. She slammed the heavy coffee table on its side cracking it. The living room looked like a war zone.

"Stop Kenya! Stop," Stacks yelled.

"You 'round here making babies with bitches and shit?" Kenya paused her emotional redecorating. Her breathing was still heavy. She seemed even angrier than when she first started.

"She's fucking lying!"

"Really nigga? I don't know who to believe. Her triflin' ass or your cheatin' ass!"

"Put her out of this bitch right now! Right now!" Stacks took two steps toward the staircase.

Kenya started laughing. "Yell! That bitch can hear you! YELL! HEY HOE, GET OUTTA MY DAMN HOUSE!" Kenya sounded almost like she was singing. Silence. British came down the stairs taking her precious time.

"Stacks, you gonna let her talk to me like that?"

"Let...me?"

"It's about time you knew what time it really is," British bossed up.

"I know what time it is. I'm done with this shit!"

"C'mon Kenya!" Before Stacks could even get her name out, she was halfway down the driveway into the waiting car service. He ran out behind her, but the truck screeched off. Stacks kept running and waving...the truck kept driving into the distance. Stacks ran until the truck bent the corner.

He went back into the house, upset with tears in his eyes. British wasn't expecting that reaction. Stacks grabbed his keys and left. She called me, "Lola! This bitch Kenya came all the way out here, fucked some shit up and left!"

"Whaaat?" I whispered into the phone. She called me at work with the tea. It was juicy, but I was sad for Kenya. Everything was out in the open now. Looked like British was finally going to get what she wanted.

Hours later, Stacks went back to the house and plopped down on the floor. British had cleaned up as well as she could considering. She sat next to him.

"What's going through your mind?"

"My family. My kids."

"We can start our own family." Stacks looked at her with only pain in his eyes.

"Not right now British."

"Why not? We talked about being together. We almost started a family. We love each other. What's the problem? You didn't want her to find out, but she did anyway. It's out there now."

"I love you both."

You would have thought that she'd finally got the picture. British could see exactly where she stood with him. A clearly painted picture. He had the perfect opportunity to transition into a relationship with her and it wasn't happening.

Stacks slept in one of the four guest bedrooms. British had the entire California King to herself. And it felt like it, too. Laying in that huge bed, in such a massive room made her feel cold and lonely. There was such a stark contrast from the way she felt waking up the day before.

"Did you see this shit?" Stacks walked into the room holding his phone out to her. There was a post on CelebMail's page, *BREAKING NEWS: Rapper Stacks and Wife Kenya Headed For Splitsville!* The headline was at the top of a picture of Stacks and Kenya holding hands, except there was a computer graphic zig zag breaking the couple apart. Underneath the main headline was a smaller one, *Kenya Leaves Stacks After Catching Him In Houston Home With Homewrecking Thot British!*

British didn't have the heart to read the article to see if there were any other truths to the story. Her eyes darted to the comments and saw the people were dogging her out! The same way they used to dog out Kenya about being a housewife and not being pretty enough, they were now dogging out British and being sympathetic to Kenya. The comments referenced all the guys British had been rumored to sleep with. They were naming names.

She couldn't take it. Stacks started reading the comments out loud. Every time he saw a comment with another man's name, he paused and looked at her. British told him to stop, yelled at him to stop, then left the room. His spirit grew more and more crushed. He looked at her as if to say, "This is what I cheated on my girl for?"

"Damn, at least Kenya don't have a fucked up reputation!" He yelled behind her. She slammed the door. Now, British saw what it felt like to be on the other side of the coin. She got to see first-hand how Sade, Kennedi and Stacks felt when their personal lives were broadcasted for the world to see. Everything would be under a microscope now.

She went through a period of depression. Added with the disappointment of the miscarriage, my girl was living in the twilight zone. British was like a lost puppy. Her pride was hurt, her heart was broken. Tears stained her satin pillowcases every night. She kept waiting for a phone call or a text and none came. She was back trolling his Instagram, as well as Kenya's, but their pages were silent.

I tried to get her to focus on her designs. Her career had been neglected, but was not so far gone that with a bit of focus it couldn't be revived. Now, her clients were going to be looking at her crazy. She already knew she was going to lose devoted customers who were still bringing her good money. Why would they want to be associated with a homewrecker? Why would they want her near their men?

The day British had been waiting for finally came. Lying down in her bed, staring at the TV, Stacks called. Her first instinct was to grab the phone and sit up in the bed so she could speak clearly, then she thought maybe the sexy voice would be better and slithered back down into the warmth of the sheets. Better yet, she did not want him to think she was waiting for him and he still had it like that. All of this came before the third ring.

"Yeah," she said as blandly as possible.

"I need to see you." Stacks spoke and his voice sounded broken.

"What's wrong?" Her guard was instantly brought down.

"I just...I...I need to see you."

"It's been more than a month since I heard from you. No calls, no texts. You might as well stay wherever the fuck you at."

"Lemme explain..." She wanted to hear what he had to say, but she had played this moment in her head over and over. You know how it is when you are on the outs with someone and you wonder what's going to happen. You think about the next time you see them, what are you going to do? The next time they call, are you going to answer or not? She had already bled out so much of the hurt that she could have left him alone and kept trudging forward. But the heart wants what the heart wants.

British tousled with talking to him in her mind, because she had already decided that whenever that moment came, he was not going to get the best of her. She hung up the phone. She felt like he just hung her out to dry. But hearing his voice did something to her. She missed him. Obviously, if he was calling her, he was ready to come back and create a life with her. Right? The next time Stacks called, she answered the phone, "Come over."

He had to have been sitting in the parking lot of her townhouse, that fool was ringing the doorbell in 60 seconds flat. She opened the door to a fragmented man. He knew he could be himself around her. Stacks stood in the doorway without all the regalia that usually came with Stacks the artist. No big chains, no shades, no fancy clothes, just Stacks.

He sat on the couch, slumped over, halfhearted. British sat down and put his head in her lap. He said he missed his wife. *Stab!* Kenya was not responding to him in any way. *Stab!* He didn't know what to do to get her back. *Stab!* Each sentence was a dagger in her heart.

He said his heart belonged to two women, but he was happy keeping British in the backfield. He could never be with her now after what happened. He didn't know she came with that kind of baggage.

In British's case, she couldn't lose a husband, because she couldn't get one. She had a loose reputation, a good number of industry dudes had fucked her and Stacks walked into the situation viewing her as the side chick. Why would he want a woman who played her position on the side and knew she was getting sloppy seconds in his time, attention, and truth? She damaged herself as a woman by giving her body so freely to any and every baller who wanted a piece.

She watched her friends get married, have children and build their families all around her while she toyed with time. Everybody around her was finding their happiness, settling into life. British was trying to overlook the obvious, that she was wasting her time and energy on someone who didn't want her the way she wanted him.

That brings us to where we are now. I'm staring at British who is looking over the picturesque views of the water crashing against the lush green sides of the mountainous islands, but homegirl's mind is nowhere near this paradise.

She is thinking of how much she loves Stacks and can't break away from him. He's making it easy for her by not responding to her and staying clear of her. Maybe this trip, being away from the world and him, will offer her some clarity.

Everybody has a past, but she doesn't know her worth.

## SADE

*When* we arrived at Virgin Gorda, the island where we were staying, we had to take a taxi van to our villa. It was basically a truck with the bed covered to protect us from the elements. There were cushioned rows of seats and our luggage went in the middle. This mode of transport was very islandy, very different. The locals were waving and smiling, it felt like we were home. Everyone there seemed so warm and friendly. At the villa, we were met with a personal butler, maid and chef. It was made very clear that they would see to our needs.

The villa only had five rooms which meant somebody was going to have to bunk. We would figure all of that out later. As the butler and maid unloaded our belongings, the chef walked us through the dining area and living room area past an invisible wall.

The kitchen, dining and living area were all one great room with views on three sides. The invisible wall was a plate of glass that led out onto the pool deck which then led out toward the ocean. If we wanted to sit inside the living area, we could with the invisible wall up to enjoy the view or put it down to catch the breeze and be able to walk right outside.

He showed us the hammocks and pool chairs, then invited us to a delectable chilled, coconut drink. Good thing it was coconut because I'm allergic to pineapples. I took that thing right down, I had a feeling it was going to sneak up on me.

"This place is beautiful!" Sade stated the obvious.

"Yeah, traveling, you have to be careful with accommodations. You nailed it Kennedi!" Madison said. "Well worth my last minute requested time off!" We clinked glasses to that.

"You chicas can go tour the place. This room, right here by the kitchen is mine." Sade took the first room. She didn't care what it looked like, how it was laid out or anything. She just wanted to be close to the food. It was classic Sade. She ate…and ate…and ate…and never gained an ounce. She only worked out once a year and looked amazing. Yeah, she was that girl.

I met Sade years ago at Kennedi's house. She was having a moment and needed to talk; Kennedi and I were already having a girl's pow wow. We've been cool ever since. Sade was born with a resting bitch face. Seriously. She didn't give a fuck about anything. Her skin was perfect, teeth perfect and her lips were juicy. She got her beautiful cocoa complexion from her mother. Her mother, even in her late fifties had beautiful brown skin you wanted to just bathe in.

They came from money. Not her mother, but Sade did. Her dad was an R&B legend. His hey-day was back in the 60's and 70's with classics that can hit the radio right now and everybody in the room would bust out singing. Tone deaf and all. He was a lead singer and did what they all did back in the day, start out in a group then went solo. His solo efforts sprang him to a sort of super-stardom. Lonnie Dorsett was the man. He still comes out of hiding for important shows, like performing on the Grammys and Oscars, as well as the occasional movie premier.

Sade's mom was his second wife. They had four children, and he had one or two in between. He wrote a song called "Claws" saying he had his claws in his woman and wouldn't let her go. Forty some years later, they are still married.

Anyhoo, Sade came up in the industry. It took more than a good looking face or a nice body to get her attention. She needed to see money, the flash of it all. Finding someone who had money, was easy on the eyes and with personality was hard to find. Until Drew came into the picture. Drew swept Sade off of her feet.

His hair had waves for days and dark chocolate skin against a pearly white smile that looked like it was manufactured perfectly for him. He always swore he never had braces or work done. He was a rookie receiver in the NFL, so you already know that body was ridiculous. Being a second round draft pick wasn't half bad, but it was his charisma kept his face in the cameras during the season.

His cocky attitude is probably what got Sade's attention. He was fine enough to make her panties melt! And they did, right off. They were making out when Drew used his hand to massage her down, you know where. By this point, she's like 19, 20. She had been fingered before, but never took it to the next step.

"Why are you so tense?" Drew asked, laying between her legs. He was trying to do his thang, but his little man was going nowhere.

"What do you mean?"

"Your body seems so rigid. Loosen up, Baby."

"Drew," she hesitated, "I've never done this before."

"I bet."

"I'm serious." He could tell by the tone in her voice. She was not laughing; her eyes looked right through him in all seriousness. "I'm a virgin."

"NO! Not the 'V' word. Oh, nah, man," he tried to retreat. She grabbed him and stared at him in his eyes, then kissed him gently.

"I want this."

"Are you sure?" Of course she was sure. By that point, the two had been on three or four months' worth of dates, claiming to be boyfriend and girlfriend. She had already stepped out and gotten herself an acting career. Being a big girl meant that she had to do big girl things. Sade grabbed his ass and nudged him in the right direction.

He kissed down her body, knowing exactly what to do to loosen her up. It worked. After that, Sade's nose was wide open. Drew could do no wrong. She was in love. As far as she was concerned, she was lucky enough to have found what her parents found early. They were soul mates. They saw each other as much as possible and had lots of fun when they were together.

Then Drew's fine, panty dropping ass told Sade he was on to the next. He gave her the old, "It's not you, it's me," line. Sade was crushed. What she experienced with him was great. It was like being on top of the world. When they were together, nothing else mattered…for her and it seemed that way for him, too.

While he moved on with his life, she moved onto her parents' couch. Any good mom knows the signs of heartbreak. Her mom was no different. Ms. Connie was good to pop in comedy DVD's and keep the kitchen stocked with ice cream, caramel syrup and sprinkles. They spent about two weeks pigging out, going shopping, eating, laughing and crying. One weekend, Ms. Connie invited her other daughter for support. Sade's sister was great in helping to keep the mood light and make jokes about the matter. She pointed out every wrong about Sade's ex.

Of course, Sade didn't bounce right back after those couple weeks, but she was much better off than she would have been. Sade knew she needed to be distracted to turn the tide. She already had a name, partly on her own merit in addition to being associated with her dad. So she used that to her advantage. She gravitated toward other kids in her same situation who had a little more to offer. More fame, more money, more prestige. This strategic move put her closer to becoming the household name she wanted to be.

Every guy she brought home was an industry guy. Ms. Connie harped about giving her heart to a man who just wanted to use her for who she was or wanted to get between them legs. Sade was beautiful, with a little pedigree, a little name and a little money. Coming from nothing, she was an attractive package. Most of the dudes she took a liking to were the bad boys…the rappers, the singers, the actors, the ball players. All of whom had a chip on their shoulders.

Her mom was not too proud to remind her that she'd taken a trip down Heart Break Lane before. It was almost like every time a guy sparked her interest, she could hear her mother's warnings in her head.

Being an actress, she traveled a lot for work and play. She always flew First Class or private. She had never known anything else. This particular day, she was on an early flight. One of her friends had a movie premier and Sade just had to be there. She took her seat, just minutes before the doors closed, her seat mate was already there. She nodded her head to be polite, but he was on the phone.

"Ma, I have a 24-hour shift, one day off, then four 12-hour shifts, back to back. I can't find anyone to cover all of those shifts at this late notice…I know, I know…the stewardess is giving me the eye…love you, too." He closed his phone.

"Liar," Sade teased. People were still boarding the plane. The stewardess wasn't giving him anything.

"You know how moms can be."

"I do. Just being nosey, I heard your work schedule. That's pretty rough."

"It is. I love it, though."

"What do you do?"

"I work in the E.R. harvesting organs. You know, right when someone dies…"

"STOP!"

"Listen," he turned to her, "it's really cool to cut someone open. Sometimes you have to get a saw and…"

"NOPE! Not interested."

"I'm a trauma surgeon." He laughed, she looked at him again with fresh eyes. She didn't want to seem like now she was interested in him because he was a doctor, but it was certainly a deviation from her norm. She was more intrigued than anything else. He didn't come from a flashy background, and as far as she knew, the blogs and paparazzi didn't know who he was. He was smart, funny and educated. She was almost positive he didn't have a criminal background; it would be hard to finish med school running the streets getting into trouble.

"Who, I mean, what were you doing out here in L.A.?" she asked.

"My brother lives here. He just had a baby, so all of us came out. I have three siblings and my parents came out, as well."

"There's four of us, too!" She beamed.

"My mom was crying about how hard it is to get all of her kids under one roof. She didn't want me to leave."

"Mama's boy," Sade joked.

"No ma'am. That's my brother. Now, he's the token for real. He has the only grandchild."

"Ooh!"

"Laying it on thick! What about you? What were you doing out here?"

"A friend's birthday. My parents live here as well. Now, I'm on my way to a movie premier in Chicago."

"The one with ahhh…ahhh," he snapped his fingers. "Dennis…"

"McCagle?"

"Yeah! Dennis McCagle!"

"That's the one."

"Nice. My friends call me Doc." Doc extended his hand for a shake. For the better part of the next four hours, they chopped it up. Even when Doc tried to get a nap, Sade kept talking. She had not talked to anybody like that in a long time. It was just like in the movies when the couple meets and can't get enough of each other. By the time they landed, they knew each other's whole life stories. Homeboy still hadn't asked Sade for her digits.

"Since you're in my city. Here's my card. My 24 doesn't start until tomorrow morning. So, if you want to grab breakfast, that'll be nice."

"Breakfast?"

"Yeah, I know your crew. Y'all will be out all night for sure!" They walked and talked a little while longer until they got down to baggage claim where a man in a suit was holding a sign with Sade's name on it.

Even if she had to sit up all night with toothpicks holding her lids up to make it to breakfast, she would have. Sade couldn't wait to see him again. They met at a small diner by his job. She got to see him in scrubs instead of street clothes. She told him he was cute. They conversed over scrambled eggs, cheese grits, sausage and buttered jelly toast. Before he hailed her a cab, he told her not to be a stranger.

He was surprised to get a text from her before the end of his shift that said to hit her up when he woke up after working his 24. She was going to be in town for a few days. Doc and Sade went to dinner, had drinks and then a movie. They thoroughly enjoyed themselves. Then she was off.

Over the next year, she made periodic trips to see him. It was easier that way. Her schedule was unpredictable, but very flexible versus his E.R. routine as a surgeon. He was a few years older than her, more settled and always tired and busy. He didn't have time to keep tabs on her, he got his time in whenever she made it available. They made good use of that time too.

"Dr. Rivers! Paging, Dr. Rivers!" Sade called out from the shower. He walked in the bathroom and stood there, watching her shower through the clear glass. She loved putting on a show for him in the shower.

Sade would turn all the way around facing him. Using a fluffy loofah, she rubbed herself in circles slowly. The left breast first, rinsed it off by flicking herself with water only using her hands, then she would get the right breast good and soapy. Doc was ready to do the damn thang, but she'd shake her head no. Then she'd take the loofah across her mid-drift and rinse it off slowly. Doc was butt naked by that point, walking to the shower.

He'd open the door and she would push him down on the bench inside. Sade would hand him the loofah and squat down with her legs wide open and her back facing him so he could wash her back. Then she'd stand up and bend over so he had a perfect view of her hoo-ha. Sade would snatch the loofah away from him, get his hands good and soapy, then bend all the way over, legs spread wide, so he could use his hand to wash her.

He'd be washing the coota-cat and playing with it at the same time, driving himself crazy! He always made grunting noises and bit his bottom lip. If he tried to stick a finger in, she'd slap his hand away, then bring it back. If he grabbed her ass, she'd slap his hand away, then bring it back. Oh, my girl teased him so good. Then she'd open his legs, slide him inside of her and get to work. The feeling of the water beating on her while he was deep inside her was more of a turn on. She always came quickly. Then he would stand her up and take control. He'd pick her up, put her back against the marble walls of the shower and give it to her hard. Being an actress, she was into voyeur type shit.

It was no secret that they were both sweet on each other. Doc was becoming a priority to Sade. Between gigs, she spent time with him. When he had weekends off, she spent time with him. When he worked normal shifts, she spent time with him.

By the time they hit the two year mark, she had keys to his place. She took him to meet her parents, it was evident they were getting serious. Doc was confident in the life he created for himself, having very little interest in merging their worlds or using her name for his gain. Her parents could see that, too. When she showed up with a modest four carat diamond on her left hand, her mother had a heart to heart with her.

"Are you sure you're ready, Baby?" Ms. Connie asked. The two women were sitting on a swing outside on the porch at the family home. Her mother had a pitcher of her world famous homemade lemonade and two glasses sitting on the table next to them.

"I do love him, Ma."

"I hear reservation in your voice."

"He's just so…regular."

"What are you looking for, Sade?" Ms. Connie turned to her.

"A little excitement. You know, Ma? A little more," she shrugged her shoulders. The day was a nice, beautiful cool day in L.A. Where they lived, there wasn't a lot of traffic and noise. The yard was wonderfully manicured. Gorgeous blooms of white roses, vibrant pink and red gladiolas and rows of sunflowers. Her mother loved sunflowers.

"Are you looking for someone who will keep you on your toes or someone to build a life with?"

"I want what you and Daddy have." Sade looked over at his powder blue Cadillac. Playa shit.

"Have you forgotten about Moya…and Reign?" Her mother said cautiously looking off in the distance.

"Moya was a separation baby and Reign was never confirmed as his."

"Oh, Sade." Ms. Connie laughed with a tone that almost sounded like pity. "You still don't get it, do you?"

"What's there to get? All couples go through tough times."

"Moya was not a separation baby. We weren't taking a break from each other or broken up. Your father was cheating on me. What do you think happened when he was out making his money? Your father was out performing concerts, city after city, state after state. He lived on the tour buses for months at a time. That man was fucking anything that moved!"

"Mama!"

"What? You need to hear this! You want a guy in the industry. You want the glitter and the glam and the money and the fans…this comes with the territory. Why do you think he never got Reign tested? He already knows! He just didn't want to prove it, because then everybody else would know too."

"You knew the whole time?"

"NO! Not at first. I was naïve. I was, we were, in love. When I looked at him the sky opened, birds chirped and angels sang. I traveled with him and saw the mobs of women throwing panties on the stage, trying to get into the hotel. I was traveling on the bus with him until I had Lonnie, Jr. After that, I was stuck home with babies. Who was keeping him company while I was here with my children? It sure wasn't me."

"I saw the way Moya's mom looked at him. I knew a man would be a man. I just expected him to be more," she cleared her throat, "discreet. That one didn't surprise me as much as Reign did. I went into a fit of depression over that one. One child wasn't enough to scare him straight."

"I thought…"

"You thought what I wanted you to think. I didn't want you growing up watching your mom thinking I was weak or it's ok for a man to run around on you and you stay. If you had known that growing up, you would have looked down on me, not him."

"I'm sorry you had to go through that."

"It was hard, very hard. But I don't want it to happen to you! Doc is a good guy. If you love him, it's worth a shot. Dealing with these popular guys means that many more women have their eyes, hearts and bank accounts tuned up for the possibilities. He keeps his nose clean, that's what I like about him."

Sade and Doc's wedding was quite a show. Lonnie held no punches, not to mention that due to Sade's acting and her own popularity, companies were willing to help pay for the wedding. Anything to attach their brand with fresh, rising talent. It was one of the most beautiful weddings anyone had ever seen.

After it was over, Doc scurried back into obscurity. They continued to do the long distance thing for a year. Even though they were married, things were still the same. She was still moving all over the country, doing auditions and small roles. She did them well, but just could not seem to break through the barrier into better roles. She was only cast to play supporting characters.

As Atlanta offered to host more and more film sets, Sade found herself spending more time there. The couple decided to move to Atlanta. Work was picking up where she began catching small roles in movies and making cameo appearances on reality shows. She quickly moved from a D-lister to a C-lister. Her popularity on social media kept money coming in from decent endorsements. Doc was easily able to get a job.

They were settling into life finally living together. Doc was ready to get the kid bandwagon going; Sade wanted more time to get her career to where she wanted it. She took a trip to the Big Apple to support another actress in what reviews were saying was her break out role. Since Doc had to work, he reluctantly sat that one out.

Sade ended up sitting next to a gorgeous football player. Sade felt like the gods were testing her will. He touched her gently when they spoke, effortlessly flashing his dimples. Sade thought she was going to fuck him right there in the auditorium. He kept grazing her arm and her thigh. Sade was boiling in the seat next to him.

She was good, though. She withstood the temptation. At the hotel that night, she got on the elevator and stared at herself in the mirrored walls as the door closed. A hand reached inside to catch the door. It was him, Titus McCree. When he looked up at her, he just smiled, walked over to her and grabbed her face.

They started kissing right there in the elevator. She was still brewing from earlier and her panties got soaked in 0.2 seconds. *Ding!* Titus walked backwards off of the elevator, pulling Sade with him. She fumbled for her room key, never taking her mouth from his. His shirt was unbuttoned before she got the door open. He easily slid her out of her dress and carried her to the bed.

She woke up the next morning and found his head between her legs. Titus hungrily lapped his tongue in and around all of her crevices. They went for two rounds before collapsing back to sleep.

Sade knew she didn't have any business there. With him. She felt like she just couldn't help herself. The thought that she had cheated on Doc crushed her.

In her mind, it was quick, it was over and nobody knew. She also knew better than to give Titus her number, then she justified it in her mind that if she didn't, a mutual friend would have. The industry was too small. There was only two degrees of separation between celebrities and personalities. Contacting each other was way too easy.

As you can imagine, British had to be the one to bust Sade's chops. She saw a picture of Sade sitting next to Titus at the premier.

Doc saw it too.

"It looks like you went to see Titus McCree," Doc started matter-of-factly when she finally called him.

"No, Babe! What are you talking about?"

"I saw a picture of you two together from last night." Sade had to think fast. This was something she didn't think she would have to think through. The truth was obvious, she didn't go with him, they just shoved him in the seat next to her. Thoughts from the night before flashed through her head and she felt a rush of heat.

"Yeah…well…you know, I kinda showed up at the last minute. I was able to get a seat, but not with her. I just had to take what I could get." Silence. He needed more convincing. "Doc, c'mon. When did I tell you I was coming? Just three days ago, right? It was all last minute. When I get home, I'll show you how much I missed sleeping with you."

Sade didn't have the heart to sleep with her husband after just being with Titus. That didn't stop her from giving him a world class, slow head session. Her hubs was ok, so she was ok.

Kennedi's husband, Ty called Sade and told her to get on the next thing smoking back to New York. He had a reading and wanted her to get first dibs on it. Doc was hesitant, being that Titus played and lived in New York, but he couldn't keep her hostage. Sade did just as she was told and hopped on the next flight. She knew this was going to be the break she needed. It was going to move her up the ranks.

"How can you come back to my city and not call me?" Titus asked as soon as Sade answered her cell. She pulled the phone away from her face and looked at it.

"How did you know I was here?"

"I run this bitch. This is my city. Did your man come?"

"No, but listen Titus. I can't do this with you. Ok? This is not who I'm trying to be."

"You already are. When and where do you want me to scoop ya?"

"No, Titus."

"Sade. Me sitting next to you was no accident. When I saw you there, the other night, I asked to be moved by you. Do you know I've been dreaming about eating you out since I saw you in *Another Monday*? I wanted you to kiss me and ride me like you did the dude in the movie." Sade got warm. "I wondered what you tasted like. Now I know. And I want more."

"Titus." She was losing her will. Just that quick. He could hear her voice get weaker.

"It's just you and me, Baby. You and me."

"I'm good."

"Sade, can you still feel me inside of you?"

That was it, the deal was sealed. She carried on with Titus for almost a year. It was good when they could get around to each other. He was hot for her. It made her feel nice to know somebody really lusted after her. The whole time they had sex, Titus would tell her what he was thinking when she wasn't around and how he waited for that moment. He boasted about savoring her sweet taste on his tongue. It drove her insane. It was much different than when she had sex with Doc.

Yet, the whole time Titus was talking, all she could think about was Drew, her first love. Why didn't Drew feel that way about her? What was he doing? Was she ever even on his mind? As sexy as Titus was, he could move her body, but not her heart. As smart and loving as Doc was, he could move her mind and her heart, but her body hungered for more.

Sade knew deep down that she did right to listen to her mother and marry him, but being with Titus was exciting. He made her feel like he could just devour her. Doc didn't give her that energy, which didn't take away from the fresh flowers he always bought her or the treat baskets he sent to movie sets when she was gone for more than a week. When Doc asked how her day was, he genuinely wanted to know.

And if all else failed, he had a career that would lend to a very good living over time.

Titus gave British tickets for the Atlanta versus New York game. Really, he was giving them to Sade, but he couldn't. Doc was not about to let Sade go to a New York game with one of her girls. He went to the game with her. Sade was pissed, but she couldn't show it. Interestingly enough, the tickets were for the owner's booth. He knew somebody, who knew somebody and called in a favor.

Doc and Sade watched the game. As you would think, Doc was more into the game than she was. At some point during the second quarter, Hamp Rivers, III walked in. She instantly knew who he was. Hampton Rivers was a flamboyant trust fund baby. His great-grandfather was a huge steel magnate back when the country was expanding. Buildings were going up left and right, so were Rivers' pockets. Four generations later, Hamp was still living and thriving on that money.

His father was white, but his mother was Sicilian. She had thick, jet black hair with ice blue eyes. So did Hamp. He was a male clone, except his skin was darker than hers. Maybe from sun bathing in the Mediterranean. He and his mother were always photographed together. She was the second coming of Jackie O.

He went by Hamp, he wanted to be cool with the rappers and ballers. Beyond the fact his family owned an NFL team, he was all about popular culture. It was nothing to find Hamp hanging out in strip clubs, back stage at concerts and private parties of the born wealthy and nouveau riche.

Hamp saw Sade and did a double take. Then he winked. She smiled and looked back at the game. He thought she looked familiar, but he didn't know her name. He also didn't know if she was famous or someone he had seen around.

"Who is that, down there on the front row?" he beckoned his assistant.

"That is Sade Dorsett. She acts."

"What have I seen her in?"

"Nothing you would remember, but her dad is Lonnie Dorsett…"

"From The Miles Boys. Ok…ok," he shook his head like he was putting the connection together.

Sade kept glimpsing up to see him work the room. *That's what I need right there. A man who can help me get where I'm trying to go. I'm fucking with the help,* she thought. Hamp bumped into Doc during half-time. They were bonding over ice cold brews and mini gourmet pizzas being served. Whatever Hamp said to Doc, it worked. Doc walked Hamp over and introduced him to Sade.

"Pleasure to meet you," Hamp said kissing her hand. Doc was grinning from ear to ear.

"Your husband told me he saves lives over at Atlanta Mercy. Me and my wife are huge benefactors there," Hamp looked over at Doc. "I probably paid your salary for the next five years!" Hamp joked to Doc. They all started laughing. Hamp never let go of Sade's hand.

"What do you do?"

"I'm an actress. You may have seen *Another Monday* and *Passion Principle*."

"Mmm hmmm," Hamp had seen the movies, but had no idea she was in them. He thought she played a secretary or maybe the nanny.

"Well, with a face like that, you should have been playing the lead roles!"

"Yes!" She eagerly agreed.

"Doc," Hamp said, "is it ok for me to get your wife's information? I'd love to introduce her to Lee Goldheimer. You know every movie he does smashes the box office."

"Umm, sure." Doc said hesitantly. It was such a random request, but how would he look standing in the way of his wife's dream?

"Ok, Mrs. Sade. I'll talk to my peeps and slide this on over to 'em." Hamp was really trying to be down to earth. He was easily the wealthiest person in the entire stadium.

Whatever hold Titus had over Sade was released at that moment. If Hamp hadn't winked at her, she would have believed he honestly wanted to help her. He invited her to lunch the next day. When she arrived at the restaurant, she was escorted to the wine cellar. Hamp was waiting for her.

"*Ciao Bella!*" Hamp stood up from the table and greeted her. Sade wore a beautiful hot pink flowy dress with a plunging neckline. A solid gold choker type necklace about three inches wide sat around her neck. Her makeup was simple, but radiant. It looked like she had been sprayed with a hint of gold dust.

"*Ciao*," she spoke seductively.

"It was such a pleasure to lay eyes on you last night. You looked like an angel."

"Thank you, Hamp," she looked down shyly.

"Tell me about yourself." They got to know each other. Sitting in the wine cellar, they were away from the prying eyes of other restaurant patrons. Sade waited on the magic words to fly out of his mouth, that he would put her in touch with Lee Goldheimer. The Lee Goldheimer. At this point, she was crunk just to be associated with Hamp. That already said a lot. After wining and dining, Hamp was ready to get to the reason he asked her to dinner.

"I hope you can be discreet." He stared at her. She responded in kind. "I think you are beautiful. I would like nothing more than to *help* you get to the next phase of your career. What are you willing to give me in return?"

"Hamp, you met my husband."

"And I can buy his whole life with the cash I have on me right now. My wife knows that a man like me has needs. She understands that every now and then, I like to swim in a different pond." Hamp spoke slowly as he ran his middle finger down her arm. "She's ok with that."

"My husband is not."

"But…are you?" Sade took a drink of her wine. She didn't know what to say. During the years, she had been propositioned, but never by anyone with as much clout or respect as Hamp. He really could help her get to the top.

"I think I'll pass. Thank you for a nice lunch."

"My pleasure. *Non è divertente...*you will change your mind." Sade gathered her purse and walked toward the door. Hamp grabbed her wrist and pulled her over to him. He kissed her hand, stood up and kissed her neck ever so gently. "Please consider my offer."

In the meantime, another guy got her attention. He was a singer, Tony B. They met on the set of a movie and became close. Her father asked her to help show him the ropes and keep him company on the set. She was able to negotiate a role for herself which worked quite well. Doc was excited for her, she seemed to be happiest when she was on somebody's set. They spoke every day and he sent flowers to her hotel room.

Doc flew out to see her two of the weekends she was there. The other two, she was in the bed with Tony B., her newest conquest. Titus was fighting to get some time, but she kept brushing him off, telling him her husband was spending a lot of time with her. He had no choice but to believe her, however letting her know that he was ready to see her as soon as she had even a one hour window.

Tony B. was just like Titus and Drew. Hot shit. He had singles firing up the charts and was on the scene hosting parties all the time. They posted one picture together and Sade gained 10,000 followers in one day. He was trying his hand at acting, like most of celebs test the waters to leverage their fan base to make money in other markets.

The sex was real good! He sang R&B and made love like she imagined he would when listening to his songs. They were equally attracted to each other. Living on opposite sides of the country, they had to skirt around to see each other once the film wrapped. Doc noticed that she was glowing more than usual and all she talked about was how popular she was becoming. Popularity didn't exactly equal paychecks, but she was getting close. She could just feel it.

Doc didn't question the shopping she did. She lived in the malls and at boutique stores. He didn't ask where anything came from. He was able to do nice things for her as well on his healthy salary. Especially being that neither of them had any kids. Doc treated his wife to a shopping spree and she treated him to a sexy show. Sade's ol' freaky ass loved showing off her body. She would dress up for him and perform. That was the one thing she kept sacred.

Going to a wrap party for a new season of a groundbreaking sitcom, Sade ran into Hamp. The funny thing was, they had never been in the same circles before, but this was probably the fourth or fifth time she'd seen him since his proposition.

"Sade, *come sei bella*. I knew you'd be here."

"Is that right?"

"Yep, got a little something for ya," he grabbed her by the hand and pulled her around the corner. It was cramped, but they were alone. The new, trendy restaurant was poppin'. The DJ blasted music, the lights were low and drinks were flowing. Hamp knew nobody would miss them for a few minutes.

He handed her a black box with a silver ribbon on it. Sade looked very surprised. Hamp stood behind her, wrapped his arms around hers and coaxed her to pull the ribbon. Inside she found six bracelets, three shiny platinum and three platinum with sparkling diamonds. Her mouth hit the floor.

"There's more where that came from, Sade. Much more." Hamp spun her around. She opened her mouth to take a breath and he lunged his tongue in her mouth. Instead of pushing him away, she found herself palming the back of his head.

It was so exhilarating. There they were kissing out in the open at a restaurant hoping not to be seen. And they weren't! Hamp pinned her up against the wall and kissed her wildly.

"*Mi manchi, tesoro mio!*" His hand found its way up the black sequined skirt she wore and pushed her panties to the side. At any second, someone could have come around into the little nook in the room, yet they were both excited.

"*Siete incredibile*," Hamp was on his knees in a split second. He came up after only a few minutes.

"That is just a taste. I have the whole world to offer you, Sade." Hamp's reach was far too wide for them to even attempt to meet in public. They used his guesthouse, his condo and houses in any city he had.

Doc noticed that she was starting to spend even more time away from home. True to his word, Hamp had been getting her more auditions and putting in words for her. "I can't audition for gigs at home," she'd say. Doc knew she was right.

"Why would this guy who doesn't even know you put you on like that?"

"Wouldn't you put me on...if you could?" She asked seductively. She made light of his accusations whenever they arose. Sade was careful to take care of home first.

Sade flew out to L.A. She and Hamp had already arranged to meet there. She arrived at the gate, he buzzed her in. As the chauffeur took her bags out of the truck, Hamp whisked her down to the guest house. He looked like a sexy Italian with his shirt open, gelled curls in his head and a gold chain around his neck.

"Talk to me," she whispered, "I like that."

"*Voglio fare l'amore con te, bella.*" In no time, he gently laid her on the couch and got right to business. He moved in a way that she had never known. He was so loose and fluid, his hips rhythmically pulsating on top of her. Hamp was really making love to Sade.

"*Mi fai eccitare,*" he whispered in her ear. She came instantly. Remaining in control, he turned her over, licked her from her vagina on to the crack of her ass all the way up to her neck in one, slow successive movement. Then slid himself inside of her again. "*Che cosa desideri? Sei come l'acqua nel deserto. Ho bisogno di te.*" Sade climaxed again. When they were both satisfied, he lay holding her in his arms.

"What were you saying to me?"

"Very, very sexy things."

"Like what, Hamp?" She giggled.

"Does it matter? I could have been saying, take out the trash, it stinks and you would not know because you don't speak Italian." He kissed her on the shoulder again. It was true, she had no idea what he was saying, but it got her off.

The thrill of having a man like Hamp in her pocket was better than anything she thought it would be. He was passionate, urgent and didn't mind flashing what he had in front of anybody. Tony B. let it be known that he wanted Sade, never letting on that they had already been romantically involved. Titus was still crushing shit on the field. He had a girlfriend, she was pretty and the fans loved her, but he was calling Sade every chance he got.

Who was at the top of her list? Drew. He was never far from her mind. All the guys she dated were in his likeness. Good looking with power, fame, and money. They all thrived on attention. Just like her daddy, Drew still had his claws in her heart. In all those years, she never got over him.

Any girl he claimed or he was rumored to be with, didn't hold a candle to her. Or so she thought. She always wondered what her life would have been like if he were a part of it. She thought about whether or not they would be happy. Sade just could not accept that she had been nothing more than a conquest to him. She was a stepping stone on his way up. She believed that he cared about her...just couldn't figure out where they went wrong.

Unlike the relationships with Titus and Tony B., Hamp hung in there for a while. They had been kicking it for two whole years! Except for the fact that Drew was not a part of her life, things were great.

Doc sat in his office at the hospital catching up on some paperwork. A rap at the door caught his attention. "Dr. Miles, I'd like you to meet someone." It was one of the members of the trustee board of the hospital. He was always there in one capacity or another. There was a whole wing named in honor of his wife.

"Yes, Mr. Chetzky. How may I be of service to you today?" Doc stood up. Mr. Chetzky didn't throw his weight around, he was always pleasant.

"I'd like to introduce you to Mrs. Hampton Rivers, III. She is one of our biggest benefactors." Mr. Chetzky stepped aside. Anybody else would have used their own name, but she knew the impression of her husband's family.

"My name is Lyla," she smiled. Lyla was pretty, not gorgeous as one would have thought. Modestly dressed.

"Lyla," Doc shook her hand. "I am pleased to make your acquaintance."

"Likewise, Dr. Miles. I would like to speak to you in detail about some of the work you have been doing. You are starting to make a name for yourself in the medical community." Doc smiled. "I know your work days are frantic, how's dinner tonight? 8?"

"Yes ma'am, Mrs. Rivers."

"Lyla."

"Lyla, that will be fine."

Doc arrived at the restaurant that night at five minutes to eight. He could not wait to hear what Lyla wanted to talk about. He was sure she wanted to invest in research he had been fundraising for. This was going to be an awesome opportunity. He was escorted upstairs to a private room. Lyla had not arrived yet.

"Dr. Miles," she waltzed in 15 minutes later. This time, she appeared slightly different. She looked more the type to grab Hamp's attention. Her lipstick was red and her bandage dress looked painted on.

"Lyla! How are you?"

"Well. Have you ordered?"

"Of course not. You weren't here."

"This won't take long. I have ordered a dessert. Would you like one?" She asked as the waiter brought in a decadent plate of sweets. "The brownie sundaes here are my favorite, which is why I decided to bring you here. For a celebration. This brownie is topped with rich truffle chocolate, handmade ice cream and sprinkled with 18 carat gold flakes." Doc just looked at her. He knew was worth a few couple thousand dollars.

"Why did this crazy woman invite me all the way here to eat such a preposterous dessert? You ask. We are celebrating, my divorce." Doc still could not understand what this had to do with him.

"Lyla, with all due respect..." she slid over a manila folder.

"It seems that your wife, Sade, is having an affair with my husband, Hamp. You see, I've known about his little flings and indiscretions through the years. Sade…she's different. She isn't just some skank who he fucked and threw a wad of cash at or some groupie who gave him head for tickets on the 50-yard-line. Sade is special to him."

Doc adjusted himself in the seat. He could not believe what he was hearing. It wasn't far-fetched, he'd asked his wife why Hamp was trying to help her for no viable reason. He just didn't want it to be true.

"I knew I couldn't come to you without proof. Those are pictures of the two of them in my L.A. guest home. They were taken last week, three months ago and oh, about five months ago. It's been going on for a while. I had stills printed from the security cameras."

"Damn."

"That's what I said, too. Until I remembered that according to my pre-nup, I get 5 million for every year that we have been together if the marriage ends due to adultery. And…another 15 million per child. I think Hamp forgot about the money part." Lyla offered Doc a golden spoon, he declined. She could see tears welling up in his eyes.

"I'm sorry, Dr. Miles, but I'm pretty sure this is going to be news. I didn't want you to be blindsided when the whole world finds out. I'll give you three days to figure out how you want to handle your end before I file my paper work." She took a bite. "Twelve years of a failed marriage never tasted so good."

Doc had worked too hard and too long to wild the fuck out about Sade and risk losing everything. He was a man of class. His wife would be away for another two days. That gave him time to pack his shit and leave. That's just what he did. He left a copy of the pictures on the coffee table in the living room.

Sade had lost her husband.

## MADISON

*Back* on the yacht, we were sailing the open seas. Paris poured us all drinks and we were ordered to down them before we got off.

"Whoever is the last person to empty their glass, has to drink another one!" Paris yelled loudly over the music blasting from the yacht's speakers. "And...if I see one drop of liquor spill, you have to drink another glass!" Man, when I tell you we were taking those drinks straight to the head! We knew Kennedi was going to be the last one. British pushed my cup up so some would spill. Kennedi then tipped British's cup so hers would spill too! British jumped and dropped her whole glass, spewing what liquor she had in her mouth out on to the boat. We all burst out laughing and Paris poured everybody another round of drinks.

We all put on bathing suit cover ups of some sort. Some were long and flowy, like mine and Madison's. British and Paris were barely covering their asses. British wore mess like that all the time, but for Paris, I think it was more of a cry for attention. Sade was basically wearing floss and a see through top. It didn't matter though; it looked like her cocoa skin was glistening under the Caribbean sun. We got a taxi truck and asked where we could find a restaurant with good authentic island food. He recommended this restaurant at the top of the island and made a call on his cell phone.

There wasn't a straight shot up the mountain, because it was so steep. So we had to go around and around, up and around, it was so crazy to me! The roads were tight and the drivers carried on like they were the only cars on the road.

"What the hell is going on in these here islands?" British blasted.

"What do you mean?" Madison asked.

"These damn drivers, that's what I mean!"

"They drive like you," Paris egged on. "You should feel right at home, here."

"But did you die?" British said mocking the Asian guy from the Hangover movies. We all laughed. So did the driver. We got to the restaurant and it seemed empty. The Divas hopped off the back of the truck quickly, only to stand there with blank looks on our faces.

"This place doesn't look open," Kennedi said.

"Yeah, I called dem and told da owner ya were coming," the driver winked at Kennedi. "Dey opened early just fuh ya.

"Awww! Thank you!" Kennedi gave him a kiss on the cheek.

"Der food is de best. I'll wait for ya."

We walked in and the place was deserted, with the exception of one table all the way in the corner. The owner quickly jumped up to greet us and walked us over to the ocean view side. Perched at the top of the island, the view looking down into the cay was amazing! Small boats dotted the sun dappled waters, while huge cruise ships passed in the horizon.

"I will give ya menus, but I would really like to bring ya chef's special plates," the owner said. He was a pudgy little man, who looked to be in his 50's with a bright, wide smile and dimples. Whatever business he had going on in the corner over there appeared to be serious. That was none of our concern.

"Chef's special it is," Kennedi spoke for the group without hesitation.

"Chef's special it is," I agreed. He took our drink orders...tequilas all around...and was gone.

"Have you ever wanted to push somebody off of a cliff?" Madison asked standing in the window. She walked over to admire the view. We looked at each other. She was either talking about her husband or his crazy ex.

You know that friend who really has their shit together? Madison was that friend. She seemed to always have a plan for any situation in life. I tease her all the time that while the rest of us were growing up playing with dolls, she was in her mother's heels and pearls practicing arguments in the mirror. That damn girl had an argument for everything; she was always playing devil's advocate. She had a way of making you see things from the other side of the coin which was usually her side.

She was an attorney who came from a good family. Her parents wanted her to follow in her father's footsteps and be a doctor, but law seemed to be more her passion. Besides, she had two brothers, both of whom decided to venture into medicine. As the youngest child in the house, she was spoiled, but her parents taught her how to fend for herself. She learned quickly to earn what she got. Her father had to work for what he had and taught his children to do the same.

Straight out of college, she went to law school and breezed through. She was able to land a job at a firm right away thanks to her father's extended network. She looked and dressed the part. Standing at 5'8", Madison was almost statuesque. She kept a weave down her back with beautiful bouncy curls for days. Madison knew she had something to prove and she kept herself looking right.

Competing with the white boys who had pedigree, Madison had to be twice as good and three times as sharp. Every day she strutted to the law office or the courtroom in tailored two piece skirt suits and blouses paired with Louboutins and Jimmy Choos. Her makeup was minimal, usually with a pop of color on her lips. Hues of pink and red did wonders for her light skin and high cheek bones.

She quickly realized that the partners at her firm were not trying to promote her. Madison had to move on to shine. That's just what she did. She applied to jobs at other firms and made it clear during interviews that she desired a more aggressive case load. She wanted to improve her litigation skills through the challenges of arguing cases during trial. Moving on to another firm was difficult having only two years of experience, but she conquered it.

Madison had dreams of being a district attorney and set her sights on Fulton County. Being female was going to be hard enough, but being black really stacked the chips against her. Strutting down the hallways of the courthouse, she received the usual long stares and surprised looks. The older gentlemen sometimes still could not believe a young, black woman had made it into the good ol' boys club. They could tell she was a lawyer versus being a client by her demeanor. She walked upright, looked them in the eye, smiled and barely nodded. The sleek, calfskin briefcase with a horse and carriage logo proved that she spent a mint on it.

When she met Robert, it was totally by accident, being in a relationship was the last thing on her mind. Robert was decent looking, bald head with rectangle glasses. His complexion was a few shades darker than hers, somewhere between Shamar Moore and Will Smith, handsome and a baby face like Larenz Tate. When she met him, he had on a fitted hat, t-shirt with jeans and bright colored sneakers. Not exactly what she had been used to, then again, her head had been in the books for so long, she wasn't sure what she was used to.

She had a staple of random guys. There was a maintenance man, who she literally used for odds and ends around the house. Mr. Friend Zone, the guy who truly wanted to be more, but couldn't break past a warm hug and a forehead kiss. The Homies, a group of guys she'd gone to undergrad with who partied together and were practically inseparable during football season. Mr. Plumber…well, she couldn't take him home to mama because he had no real future plans, but he laid pipe the way she needed it. Mr. Backfield, he was the guy who she called, when Mr. Plumber couldn't be reached and she needed to be worked out. Mr. Backfield was also good for dinners and movie dates.

Madison was good, so when she met Robert at an album listening party, her roster was already full. With a catch like Madison, her whole roster played at their full potential. All of them wanted to be available when she decided to settle things down a bit. She went with a lawyer friend who practiced entertainment law, Monica. The restaurant, turned event venue was downtown and apparently was the spot for many intimate gatherings from wedding receptions to birthday parties to…you guessed it, listening parties. An intimate crowd of about 100 people were there to hear the new album, it was a good sized crowd to mingle in. As it turned out, Robert was a record industry exec. He found and produced talent, including the artist who was presenting that night.

He couldn't help but want to step to her. She was classy and kept it simple. Rocking tight jeans, and a loose silk shirt, Madison was turning heads. He appreciated her minimal makeup in a world where women felt like they couldn't leave the house until they accomplished a geisha look. Stilettos completed the outfit and she knew how to walk in them. He saw a few guys open up a conversation with her just to obviously be turned down, because he saw them walk away trying not to look defeated.

"You know, I'm not like these other guys around here. I know exactly who you are."

"Is that right?" Madison challenged. She knew exactly who he was too and would be totally impressed if a man of his caliber knew who she was.

"Yes ma'am."

"Ok?" She stared at him waiting on him to saying something lame, sure that he was used to having girls throw themselves at him.

"You are the girl waiting on me to come over and ask you what's yo' name and what's yo' sign!" Madison rolled her eyes, bothered. *Damn, even worse than I thought.* She turned on her heels to walk away.

"No, no, no." Robert grabbed her arm to keep her from walking. She looked at him thinking, *whatever else you have to say better be good, buddy.* "Madison Taylor," he said laughing.

"Look at you!" She did the slow clap.

"I read the article about you in Upward Atlanta magazine."

"You remembered my name?"

"Honestly, no. I remembered your face, because I remember thinking how pretty you are. I got your name from Monica."

"I'm a little tied up tonight with the listening party, but I would love the opportunity to sit and chat with you over dinner."

"I think I'm good."

"Cool, no pressure. Here is my card, call me *when*…you change your mind." Robert gave her a card that simply had his name, email and phone number. The email address was his first and last name at gmail. Very generic. Even though he was a very successful A&R, he was clearly not caught up in titles. Or he knew anybody he was giving his card to already knew who the hell he was.

It only took a week before she was bored enough to call him. He lingered in her mind and seemed to be genuinely interested beyond the cliché 'you're fine, I wanna holla' dudes. Madison was in the mood for a different type of company. He took her for tapas in Virginia Highlands. Easy vibe, no expectations and she could eat without acting like she had to starve herself.

Madison was very surprised at how easy it was to talk to Robert. Before either of them knew it, they were closing down the restaurant. They had nothing in common, but the conversation came so easily. Neither of them dominated and their personalities gelled so well. In no time at all, they were spending hours a day on the phone or hanging out. Madison put no pressure on him to put a label on what they had, they were just enjoying themselves. She was happy to have company, and he didn't mind having a smart, beautiful girl on his arm.

Madison got busy with work. The tougher cases she wanted required more dedication and longer hours. She was ok with that, she knew the grind would pay off in the end. Robert respected her hustle as he had one of his own. He was always traveling around the country in the market for new talent, yet he made time for her. When their demanding schedules did not allow them to see each other for days at a time, he made sure to connect with her over the phone.

The relationship between them blossomed and Madison began spending less and less time with her team. Robert was filling all of the voids and what little spare time she had. He'd try to pry her to get information about cases that he knew she couldn't discuss and she would divert his attention to his up and coming artists. They enjoyed each other's company. They did everything from summer concerts to art galleries, when possible.

Robert's job took him out to L.A. for a few months. He would be gone for a while and Madison knew she would miss him; however, the easiest thing for a lawyer to do is occupy time. There was never a shortage of briefs, testimonies and research to do. He asked her to save herself for him; she laughed and said she wouldn't make any promises. After a month, they were both feeling it.

"I miss you, Madison."

"Ummm, you're being weird," she joked. She really missed him too.

"C'mon, man. It's been forever since we were able to hang out. I'm out here in sunny L.A., all by myself. Lonely. No one to talk to. Wishing you were here." He purposely tried to make his voice sound sad.

"I wish you were here in Atlanta with me."

"You can be here…ya know?"

"Robert, you'll be alright. I cannot spare the time to break away and fly cross country."

"Dang, it's like that?"

"You're supposed to be out there for work, so work. Do you know how long the flight is from the East to the West Coast?"

"Yes ma'am. I make the flight often."

"Are you aware what an encumbrance it is to attempt to study briefs on the plane's tiny pullout tray? Do you know that performing research using resources limited to that of an iPad would drastically decrease the chances of...

"I need to see your pretty face."

"...would drastically decrease the chances of...."

"I'll have my assistant buy you a ticket for Friday. Pack a bag, you are coming to see me."

"I can't just..."

"Yes you can! You deserve a break. I'll take you to all of my favorite spots out here." His voice sounded so energized.

"Well, I haven't been to L.A. before." Madison didn't give herself a chance to travel and see anything. This trip would be new and out of the ordinary.

True to his word, by the end of the day, there was an airplane ticket with Madison's name on it. She was impressed with how quickly Robert moved. A part of her didn't believe he was going to send for her, so she didn't think about packing her bags until she got the flight confirmation.

When they saw each other at the airport, it was evident they were giddy with excitement. Madison was trying to keep from running, she was so excited, she just couldn't help it. He grabbed her in a tight embrace, spun her around and kissed her. It felt so good to be in each other's arms again.

"This is what I wanted you to see," Robert said walking through the sliding glass door of the house to the infinity pool. He had a house in the Hollywood Hills. He walked her to an oversized, round patio chair, sat down with his legs open and put her in between. Leaning back on him where they sat, the view was pristine. Madison could see a plethora of lights down in the valley and out into the city. The world was alive, but all they could hear was the faint sound of wind as it whistled through the trees. And each other's heartbeat. The sun danced into deep oranges and plums on the horizon. It was incredibly peaceful.

"O...M...G! This is absolutely amazing! It's like nothing else exists."

"But you," he swooped her hair out of the way to kiss her neck ever so gently. The gusts of wind sent a chill down her spine. Her body opened up in a way she had not expected. She tilted her head and grabbed the back of his neck to let him know he was welcomed there. They craned around until their lips met and they hungrily explored each other's mouths.

She stood up and undressed in front of him. Slowly, pants first, then shirt, followed by her bra. He shook his head no and pointed to her panties. Madison giggled and pulled her panties down, then back up, then down again. They both laughed. Once they dropped to the floor, he admired her body. He had seen her in skin tight clothes, but what he saw was even better than he anticipated. She walked to the edge of the round patio chair and pulled his pants off from the cuff. Robert made sure his boxers went with them.

Madison straddled him and they kissed passionately. Robert's throbbing boomerang made her get so wet. So did knowing they were outside and at any point, any of their neighbors could come out and have somewhat of a view of what they were doing.

She was so excited, little foreplay was needed. Even wearing protection, he slid right in. She took her time riding him slowly, thrusting him with her arms wrapped around his neck. Then she pushed him back so he could slide deeper into her wetness. She moaned and grabbed her own breasts because that shit felt so damn good. Seeing that she enjoyed herself so, Robert climaxed immediately. Madison placed tender kisses all over his body as they embraced each other under a setting sun in the L.A. sky.

Robert was fun and outgoing. Of course, because he had money, he was able to keep up the high maintenance lifestyle she had somewhat become accustomed to with a good job, but he always managed to do little things. He bought her flowers, he even took her to find the best chocolate chip cookies in the city. One day, they went on a mojito hunt. They spent the day going to different restaurants sampling mojitos to see who had the best one. The main thing was how they were enjoying each other's company.

As a just because gift, Robert bought Madison a passport holder. She didn't even know what it was. She opened the box and gave him a half ass smile, followed by a, "Gee, thanks." He told her they were going to push beyond the states to see some shit. When Robert and Madison took their first international trip, there were still no labels on the relationship. They flew to London and Dubai, places she had only seen on TV, as well as Valle de Guadalupe, and other places she had never heard of because she was so busy working toward an award winning career. Without the pressure of labels, they were fully aware that the other person was there because they wanted to be. Nothing was keeping them there, legally or out of obligation.

For her 29th birthday, Robert took her to a beautiful Spanish restaurant off the grid. It was located amongst historic houses downtown. In a small, intimate setting, the yard was decorated to look like old world Spain with rows of hanging lights and small tables with vivid tablecloths. Robert hired a band with a professional singer and invited a few of Madison's good friends, me and The Divas included.

We were having an awesome time. Talk about food! There was so much food! It seemed like plate after plate of Spanish family-style dishes adorning the table. After we all ate and were sitting around drinking, the music died down. We all could take a hint. We knew something big was about to happen, Madison on the other hand, did not catch on at first.

"Is dere anything else ju would lie ma'am?" A waiter asked Madison.

"No, I think I'm good."

"Wine? Sangria?"

"Yes, I'll have another sangria."

"What about dessert?"

"Not for now, in a little bit," we couldn't believe she was carrying on a conversation and hadn't noticed that Robert had disappeared from her side.

"Will you accept Robert's proposal?"

"Huh?!" The waiter turned Madison's chair around and Robert was behind her on his knees holding a box with a ring. She was stunned! She started crying and laughing at the same time. It was a simple classic round solitaire on a platinum band.

She was never against the idea of marrying, she wanted it done the right way. Here again, she had put no pressure on Robert. He asked her to marry him in his own time when he was comfortable. Her immediate answer was, "Yes!" Over the course of the next few days and weeks, she had to really consider what they were about to do.

Talking about their futures, they shared intimate pictures of what they envisioned for their lives. Robert already had three children from a previous marriage. He and his ex, Shelly were the fortunate divorcees who realized that kids suffer more in divorces than parents. They worked hard to keep lines of communication open and honest. Shelly didn't use the children as pawns to piss him off because they were no longer together. Robert made sure he was there for them emotionally, as well as financially.

With him already having three kids, Madison was content having just one or two of her own. She was particularly close to his oldest, a teenage daughter named Desiree. They spoke on the phone often and hung out doing cool step-mom or big sister type shit.

Desiree's mom was glad Robert found someone mature enough to handle her and the kids. Madison and Desiree went to movies, got mani pedi's and gave Desiree's mom a break from the teen 'tude.

"Desiree!" Madison answered her cell when it rang. Obviously, she had caller I.D.

"Ughhhhh Madison!" the teenager screamed in the phone. "Mama won't let me go to the movies this weekend with Vic! Can you talk to her? Please! He's soooo fine and he wants me to go to the movies with him. Mama is trippin'!"

"Hmmm, Hi Madison. How was your day at work? Did you win any cases today?" Madison mocked to show her teenage step-daughter how the call should have gone. "My day went well, thank you. How was your day, Desiree?"

"Fine!" she laughed. "Will you help me puh-leeze?"

"Sure, I'll talk to your mom. But first, tell me a little bit about this boy." Madison and her step-daughter were close. At 13, Desiree felt like she needed someone to go to bat for her. Luckily, Madison and her mother were mature enough to have a good relationship for the sake of the kids. They weren't BFF's, but they were cool. It also helped when her mom felt like she couldn't reach Desiree to have a go between who she knew had everybody's best interests at heart.

Madison was tickled at the thought of seeing what a little person mingled with her own DNA looked like. Allowing herself the freedom to see that having a family was a real possibility, she recognized that she did want to have her own kids.

Madison had not previously allowed herself to give much thought to having a family. Opening her eyes, she saw the writing on the wall. She felt like her options were to have a career or have a family. As a woman, it was hard to do both. If she wanted to be successful and have a career, she had to get the ball rolling early to see longevity. It would be too hard to launch a career while trying to have children at the same time. The women she saw around her either had children young and struggled to grasp at the career they dreamt of or they were very successful and clamoring to find a husband and have kids before their clocks ran out.

Now that she was engaged, she had to decide what her choice was going to be. She was already knocking on 30 and had done well so far by staying focused getting her career on track. Madison Taylor was fierce in the courtroom while gaining popularity in her new position. It felt good to have the support of her man behind her. Madison applied to the Fulton County District Attorney's office and earned a position as a Deputy District Attorney. She was only two steps away from being the District Attorney, although those steps may as well have been giant leaps across mountainous canyons.

Having a fiancée by his side, Robert was living in a dream. He was happy that he found someone who he felt genuinely loved him for who he was, not what he could offer. The security of the commitment made him cling to her even tighter.

That bitch. Out of nowhere, Lady Soul blasted up the scene with news of a tell-all book that she had written. Lady Soul was a widely popular R&B singer/songwriter who did more songwriting than singing. Her style evolved with time and after 20 plus years in the industry, she could still pen a top 10 hit in her sleep! She was known for glorifying natural hair and wore amazing two-strand twists, bantu knots and knot outs.

Lately, she encouraged a healthier lifestyle. In addition to her newfound adoption of a conscious, green lifestyle, she spoke about purging the heart, mind and soul. Part of her purge was to empty her soul into a tell-all book that, according to her publicist, was going to shake the industry. The buzz surrounding it said it would talk about her transition from B-girl to free spirit. She often spoke about higher vibrations and positivity.

Lady Soul was no video vixen telling her side of the music industry, this was coming from a respected veteran dishing about all the sex, drugs and rock n' roll type shit people dream about when they imagine a life in the industry. The industry held its breath, so to speak, until the first print hit the shelves. Nobody knew what to really expect. Not only was it a tell-all, but she had the nerve to name names!

Lady Soul's relationship with Robert was front and center; along with other men she had been with. She made accusations that she had been in an abusive relationship and named Robert as her abuser. She even went further to discuss, in detail, how he forced her into threesomes and orgies, while their relationship was plagued with drug use and alcoholism.

Madison and Robert were completely blind-sided by the news. Madison was aware that Robert used to date Lady Soul, although the ladies had never actually met. Lady Soul's anger towards him seemed to stem from news of the engagement when it finally hit.

True or not, it was out there. The public did not see Robert that way. He was well off and had his children with him often, but a womanizer and drug abuser were far from the radar.

It was no military secret that Robert and Lady Soul were in a relationship together. They were both very successful at their crafts and worked together behind the scenes jumpstarting well-known artists careers. Robert was never seen with bum bitches. They all had something going for themselves. But no one had ever seen signs of abuse. Ever.

I, personally, feel like she's a woman scorned. For whatever reason they broke up, Lady Soul was not over Robert and did not want him walking anyone else down the aisle. Madison was beautiful, obviously smart and had a career to envy. Lady Soul was not having it.

When the news of Robert being named as an abuser broke, his bosses at the record label called him in for an emergency meeting. He booked a last minute flight to L.A. for them to berate him with questions.

He walked into a room surrounded by glass that frosted over at the flick of a switch to keep nosey asses out of their business.

"Robert, what the hell is going on?" David spoke first. He was a balding, fat guy who created the label with money his father gave him. His livelihood was immediately at stake.

"I don't know where this crazy bitch is coming from with this."

"Well, somebody needs to figure it out. I don't like it. I don't like it one fucking bit!"

"How the fuck do you think I feel?"

"I don't really care how you feel. Did I ask you how *you* feel?" David spoke pointedly.

"What we need to know is…did you do any of it?" Rosen asked. He was David's right hand man. They grew up together and were closer than brothers. Rosen was the 'good cop'.

"NO! I didn't hit her ass. I never hit her ass…I mean, I hit it. You know, we had sex, but I didn't abuse her. I don't know why she's making this shit up!"

"Is there any proof to back her up anywhere?"

"No!"

"No pictures…no friends who may have seen you two fighting…no police records?"

"Nothing!"

"Apparently she has an ax to grind with you." Rosen had done his research. His ears had been to the ground since her first social media post about the book coming out. He was so well connected it wasn't hard to get news. They just didn't know it was going to be all bad for Robert.

"She doesn't have to make up lies and shit about me to sell this damn book!"

"She needs a story, something that will stir up fresh interest in her as an author. This is a new side of her. The public knows her as a singer and songwriter, not as an author."

"Can't we gag her? Gag…order?" Robert asked, David and Rosen laughed.

"From saying your name? Sure. But the damage is already done and she will just keep saying, 'my manager' and it will be implied. Even if we remove every single book from shelves in stores, that won't take it out of the homes and off the iPads of those who have already purchased it." Robert and David shook their heads agreeing. The air in the room was thick with frustration as they sat in silence, all of them thinking.

"Robert," David said standing up with all seriousness, "get in front of this shit. I don't care who the train hits, as long as it's not me. Quit gallivanting across the globe with this new girl of yours. Sniffing up her ass is not going to pay your bills. Find me some fresh talent! We need to blow Lady Soul out of the damn water."

Robert left feeling like he had been threatened. The tone was not what he was expecting. He knew he needed to come up with a plan. He just hoped that Madison would be behind whatever it was he decided to do.

When he got back to Atlanta, the weight was still heavy on him. He was not expected to be welcomed to the city with blog reporters bombarding him at the airport asking about Lady Soul's accusations.

This was not at all how he thought this situation was going to affect him. Not to mention the social scene in Atlanta was too small, he knew he would run into Lady Soul eventually. He had to strike, hard and fast to rain on her parade. She could eat without taking food from his plate. There was enough to go around.

He drove straight from the airport to Madison's condo. They needed to talk. She was happy to see him, although not as excited as usual. This was weighing heavily on her as well. She walked him over to the island in her kitchen.

"I think I have a solution to this whole Lady Soul thing," he started. Madison shook her head that she was listening. "We just have to talk; have a united front."

"No."

"Listen, Baby, I have been in the industry for a long time. I know the ins and outs of how things work. By coming out with it, she's already given me a platform to clear my name and bring in more artists."

"You don't need to do that. We can find another way."

"Like what?" Robert asked irritated. "You didn't even give my idea a single thought before you dissed it."

"I did, but I just don't think that's the way to go about handling this. You hopping on those interviews will just continue to feed into this bullshit. It'll be easy for them to take your words and use them against you. You know that producers air what they want to air for ratings. I sure as hell don't need to be out there like that. You shouldn't want your kids exposed to that. Watch, next week, everybody will be on to something else. This shit will die down. Don't worry about it, Babe. It will be gone after she gets her little fifteen seconds."

She walked around to the side of the island where he was standing and kissed him. He turned his head so she kissed his cheek. She could see that her man was in pain, but she spoke from her heart believing that things would pass. She wrapped her arms around his waist and continued pecking him on his neck and down to his chest. Madison rubbed up and down his body trying to ease his frustrations.

Robert picked her up and sat her on the island. He looked into her eyes and she could see the enormity of what he was feeling. Without any words, they stared into each other's eyes, both of them yearning to be understood, aching to be trusted.

They continued to plan their wedding waiting on Madison's anticipation of the next big thing to ring true. Robert and Madison did the do, in an elaborate intimate setting. There was so much love in the place it was almost unreal. As pictures of the wedding surfaced, Robert and Madison became household names. With the stunt Lady Soul pulled, she only brought attention to the new couple and people began digging into Madison's life.

The public fell in love with her and were happy for them as a couple. Madison was the type of girl that all the hustlas wanted. She was pretty, very smart and driven. She had a real career and seemed to hold her man down when shit was hitting the fan. The drama was bringing more attention to Madison's career and stealth legal abilities. As a record exec, Robert was a hustla. The music industry was fickle, the fans had little loyalty to artists until the artists proved themselves. It was Robert's job to give the fans something to love and hold on to.

Lady Soul put on a huge book launch all around the country. She also engaged in speaking opportunities and used it all to broadcast more fallacies. She took advantage of Robert and Madison's blissful wedding to concoct more stories of Robert abusing her. She went on and on pointing the finger at him and making accusations of emotional pain.

The spectacle unleashed by Lady Soul seemed to be counterproductive. The more shit that spewed out of her mouth, the more Madison and Robert were able to use it to their benefit. The public really saw it as jealousy. It seemed like Lady Soul was just hating on their happiness.

Then slowly, the tide started to turn. When Lady Soul didn't let up, people had no choice but to listen. She talked about it on social media, on talk shows, at her half-ass cameos at concerts. Everywhere she had a platform, the topic of Robert abusing her came up. Tears and snot-nose antics seemed to give truth to what she was saying. The public view turned to thinking that if she was still talking about it, it must be true.

Robert's money was finally becoming affected. People were becoming more hesitant to do business with him because of the notoriety that came with beating women. He wasn't comfortable just sitting at home doing nothing. They both had seen relationships where men let their women take care of them because they didn't have a pot to piss in or a window to throw it out of. Nor did the guys care! Her husband was not that guy. He was used to being a provider, taking care of his children and himself with money to burn. Even before he had record exec money, he grinded hard to provide for his first wife and their kids. Robert talked to Madison again about coming forward to speak against it and she said no.

"I got your back, Robert. We will get through this!"

"Why can't I defend myself? People are blowing me up to be on TV and radio shows. How hard is it for me to go and speak? You don't have to say anything. The public loves you! Just be there with me to show support. That would be nice. You *are* my wife."

"You don't need to feed into that. I just think it's a bad idea for you to get involved."

"A bad idea? She is publicly bashing my name. The shit didn't pass like you said it was going to! Now, I'm losing money! People don't want to work with me. How am I going to take care of you with no money coming in?"

"You still have your job," Madison tried to use a sensitive tone. "We are in this together, Baby. I'm telling you, she can't keep up with this shit much longer."

"Do you have any idea what this feels like? To be alienated, questioned and have niggas steady pointing their fingers at me when I walk around the mall and shit?"

"Nigga, you can miss me with that shit! Don't think you are in it by yourself! People at the job have slick shit to say to me, especially the black ones making it their business to spread this trash around. My family calling and texting me, Lady Soul this and Lady Soul that. Fools from junior high school hitting me up on Facebook, too! I just don't let it bother me! You are better than that, Baby. Let's focus on us, what's really important. Let's get to baby-making!" Madison said with a devilish grin.

"Baby-making? That's what you're worried about? Get your head in the game, Madison. You always have a plan, you are so strategic when it comes to your career. Now, since you don't like my plan, come up with one of your own. Maybe you really don't care because it's not your career at stake falling through the cracks."

The next morning, Madison woke up and Robert wasn't in the bed with her. She never felt him get up out of the bed. She laid there listening to the sounds of an empty house to hear if he was in the shower or downstairs. Silence.

She received a text from British commending Robert for finally breaking his silence. When Madison asked what she meant, British told her to turn to WSIT for the morning show.

"Welcome back to WSIT, The Streets Is Talking!" The lively male voice spoke, "Today we got Robbie Cool in the building! That's right people, Mr. Robert Wimbley, responds to accusations that he abused Lady Soul in her tell-all book that surfaced last summer. And he does it here first! Call all ya friends and tell them to tune in, they do not want to miss this!"

Madison's heart sank. She was hurt that he had gone to the radio show to do exactly what she asked him not to. Then on top of that, he did it without even telling her. She felt betrayed and figured he had already made arrangements to talk before they had the conversation the day before.

Tension in the house grew by leaps and bounds. The days of careless fun and endless laughter seemed to be more of a stretch. Robert was preoccupied with what was becoming of his public image and financial future. The first interview led to many others. He hit up all the stations in metro Atlanta in one day! Then he began traveling to big cities like L.A. and New York.

Lady Soul finally kicked up enough dust to land an interview on one of the national morning TV shows and used it as a platform to further exploit her version of the relationship that took place between her and Robert. She wasn't even publicizing the book as much as she was broadcasting her made-up emotional and physical abuse.

The producers of that same national morning TV show approached Robert wanting to use her interview as a chance to let him defend himself to millions of viewers. He was excited, he didn't have to go to them, the opportunity fell in his lap. He couldn't wait to present it to Madison.

Robert felt like with the producers coming to him, he would have a more fair chance at representing his side, versus him asking to be on the show. He could finally make an effort to clear his name with millions of people watching. Madison insisted she not be involved.

"Come on, Madison! You gotta give me a break!"

"Robert, I am a Deputy District Attorney for Fulton County. Do you understand what kind of weight that carries? You are already out there doing your thing! It looks like you're doing it fine without me." Madison was throwing shade. "I cannot be involved in those kinds of shenanigans. What you do is a direct reflection of me now. That doesn't mean I have to support it. This can end my career, too. Then where will we be? Who will take care of us and our kids then?"

"We don't have any kids!"

"We will."

"Not unless you are going to pay to reverse this vasectomy!" *BOOM!* That was a blow she was not expecting. In all of their talks about the future, never once did he mention he got a vasectomy when his first marriage ended. He always went right along with her talking. Whenever Madison wanted to get started having a baby was fine with him, he said. He had not planned to tell her that way, but emotionally, he just exploded.

Robert was furious! He started to resent her. Initially, by being silent about the accusations, he was honoring her wishes, keeping somewhat of a peace in the home. At the same time, he felt like Lady Soul was getting a pass to say whatever she wanted about him and her petty ass was dogging him out. It also seemed like he had something to hide.

When he started talking, his wife didn't support him defending himself. That, too, became a topic of discussion. How could a married man come forward to dispute rumors that he is an abuser and his wife *not* stand in the court of public opinion to show her support?

People did not feel at ease about that at all. Madison's lack of support did not reflect badly on her, as much as it reflected badly on him. It further gave credibility to Lady Soul's claims. What kind of wife doesn't stand by her man in tough times? One who doesn't believe in him. He lost respect from his friends and peers. Ultimately, that led to artists not wanting to work with him and the most feared of all…he lost his job.

Riding the wave of emotion, Robert went from furious to devastated. He wanted so badly for Madison to see this situation from his point of view. She didn't seem to. She wanted to protect their new marriage and the career she had worked so hard for. How could Madison have known that this story would trail on this far?

In the meantime, opportunities kept coming to Madison as a result of the press digging into her past. She landed in Black Enterprise Magazine's '40 Under 40', a coveted list of young, black movers and shakers. She was being asked to do speaking engagements, for a fee of course. Her bosses also saw that she was not allowing her personal life to interfere with her winning record. The girl was 25-1. She was becoming a shark in the courtroom.

Madison didn't think about the long term affects this could have on Robert. Unfortunately, shit just wasn't coming together for him.

"Do you even care that my shit is all fucked up?" Robert asked Madison in anger one day.

"What kind of question is that? Of course I care."

"You don't seem to. All you care about is what's going in your pocket…you making money!"

"Do you know how hard it was for me to get where I am? Do you have any scope of the sacrifices I have had to make to have even a *glimmer* of a chance at an illustrious career? This isn't something that just anybody can do, Robert! I can't even speed on the highway, without fearing it will make the 6 o'clock news. I have had to sharpen my skills and study my ass off at the expense of a personal life. I spent days with no sleep, living on coffee and peanuts just to give myself an edge over my competition. I can't count the number of times I have been the only black face or the one person in a skirt. You can't imagine the types of nappy headed, slave bitch jokes and discrimination that have been thrown at me. But you think I don't care?"

"You don't! You made that clear!"

"What do you want me to do? You want me to stop working? How are we gonna pay bills then?"

"Support me Madison! I listened to you when you had me looking like a coward...a punk ass nigga who beats women and didn't wanna confront it! I held my peace until I couldn't any more. I'm out here clearing my name without my wife. How credible do I look saying I don't hit women and my own wife is *never* by my side?"

"This shit is embarrassing, Robert. Honestly, I don't feel like taking off work to deal with this sess pool of shit swirling around Lady Soul's stupid ass. I don't understand why out of all the guys she's been with, you are the one who gets all the negativity."

"Fuck this," he mumbled under his breath walking away.

"What?" Madison scrunched up her face and cocked her head to the side. She knew his slick ass comment was directed towards her.

"I said," he cleared his throat to make sure she heard him, being a complete asshole. "Fuck...this! I was honoring your wishes to keep peace in the home, you didn't do the same. Now, what peace do we have? Yes we are married, but if you and I don't make it, this is still my life. And the lives of my kids. I am the one who has to live with this Lady Soul bullshit. Not you! You seem to have forgotten that. My whole livelihood has been caught up in her dumb ass fantasy world. A nigga lost his job, friends, all streams of making money. I was in high school the last time I was broke. That was 20 years ago!"

"Sue the bastards," his wife suggested.

"Huh?"

"Sue them. Sue Lady Soul and sue the publisher of the book allowing her to defame you like that. I have a few friends in entertainment law who will put the wheels in motion. Monica! She does entertainment law! Let me make a call." Finally somewhat happy with a resolution, Robert got the ball rolling to place a lawsuit on those involved. This would shut Lady Soul up, compensate him for the loss of past and future earnings and show effort to clear his name.

Suing them still did not make up for the fact that his wife did not have his back. He felt like if anybody was going to jump at defending him, it would be his wife who earned a living defending the law. She was a pro at it!

Their situation went from bad to worse. By the time the lawsuit was filed, the situation had dragged on for nearly two years. The owners of the book publishing company were so heavily connected in the music industry, Robert was completely blackballed. No one would work with him, no one wanted to hear his side of anything.

At one point, she found Robert crying on the back patio, sitting by the pool. Not the sobbing, snot-running cry, but the emotion was so much that tears streamed down this face. He was so overwhelmed, he truly felt the weight of the world on his shoulders. She sat down to comfort him and he flinched. He looked at her and slid away from her. She slid over to where he was. He stood up and looked down at her.

"You know, Madison, you never asked me if I did it."

"So…what does that have to do with anything?" She answered. Being a lawyer, she knew exactly where he was headed with it.

"You didn't ask if I had abused her because you never had the intention of defending me or supporting me or going to bat for me." With that said, he walked back in the house.

Madison felt some kind of way about him blaming her for how it unfolded. She pushed back. In actuality, they were pushing away from each other. Madison was spending more time with her friends and Robert was out of the house half of the time. If he was home, he was not anywhere near her. They were both losing sleep over the state of their relationship. There was little to no communication. In truth, they were spending more time talking to themselves than to each other.

Madison was now the sole breadwinner and she was holding it down financially. She never thought she would have to help a man get back on his feet. Robert could not get a job, he could not be himself, he had no peace, all because of how selfish she was for never making a public appearance to stand beside him. When the pastor said, "For better or worse," neither of them was expecting this. Madison was not prepared for how bad the feelings associated with 'for worse' could be.

They sunk to their lowest low. They barely saw each other and hardly spoke to each other because an argument broke out, literally, within minutes. They could be talking about the weather and it would end up about Lady Soul. That is not the way either of them wanted to be. They were both hurting.

Madison was in the process of losing a husband because of her unwillingness to compromise and realize that she was not in the relationship alone. She now made more money than him and put her career before him and his well-being, not seeing that it was hurting them as a couple.

Madison was not willing to listen to what he had to say. She heard him, but she wasn't really listening. She was unsupportive, even when all he asked for was her presence. Robert should have had more input in the situation because although they were married, Lady Soul's accusations affected him more. His vote should have been the deciding one. Instead, Madison was hell bent on having things her way. She was selfish. She should have given her opinion, but let him handle it the way he saw fit.

Robert moved out. He told her he felt stifled and needed to find himself. The energy between them was so bad, he couldn't do that with her around. Madison got scared, thinking, *Am I about to lose my husband for real*? She didn't want him to leave, but there was no changing his mind. She really didn't try to. At the point when she saw him packing bags to leave, her pride and her heart were damaged.

Robert began acting out, seeking attention. Since he was in such a bad place with his wife, he acted out on social media. He posted pictures of crazy shit, telling Madison he was concentrating on a hobby. From the looks of things, he was getting into other women moreso than a hobby or finding himself. She didn't feel that married couples should separate. Her mind grew wild with dark, twisted fantasies of what he could be doing with other girls when she was not around. Seeing him have freedom made her feel even more selfish than before.

While he was out soul searching, she had to think about whether or not she wanted to even be with him. When she wrote out a list, the pros outweighed the cons. She had to realize that in his life, he was the star and his light had become drastically diminished in her shadow. He would have been ok with that if she had allowed him to shine in the home which she didn't allow him to do. Rather than let him be a man, she questioned every choice he made, every decision he believed in.

Through it all, they have opted to go to counseling. Giving up is easy, fighting for your marriage to make it through those 'for worse' moments is when you see what you are both really made of and if it will last.

## KENNEDI

*Later* that night after getting back to our villa, Kennedi suggested that we chillax by the pool. I must admit, we were a cute group of chicks. All my Divas had fresh manicures going on, no dry, cracked feet. Me and Paris trotted down to the beach, I wanted to check out that big ass hammock just feet from the water.

We saw a white lady with cornrows and beads on the end, you know, the kind tourists get when they travel to the Caribbean. She immediately approached us, smiling a mile wide.

"Hey ladies!" her accent was a strong, English one. I guess she could tell by our reaction that we were somewhat stunned by it. "Yah, I know, I know. The locals have been laughing at me, it's ok." We couldn't help laughing either.

"We were just..." Paris started, but couldn't finish.

"We weren't expecting it," I said.

"Yah," she laughed. "The name's Daphne. I'm staying in the next villa. Well, actually, me and my crew."

"We are on a girls' trip too!" Paris chimed in. I looked at her with the sly stank face and my eyes grew slightly wider, like *Bitch, we don't know her. This could be a setup.* You always have to keep your guard up!

"We'll be making a ton a noise. I wanted to invite you ladies to our bon fire. I have my children, husband and about 30 other people with me. We rented all of the other villas on this property, and we're a rowdy bunch!" There were only four villas total. I knew how much we paid for ours, so I was quickly doing the math. "It's gonna be fun. Go get your girls!"

"I'll ask if they want to come," I began.

"Let me go introduce myself." Daphne blasted past us up the trail with Paris and I in tow. She introduced herself to everyone and their faces were

crazy! Like, *where did y'all get this white lady from?*
It seemed innocent enough. We grabbed our shoes and
walked down to the bon fire. Most of her crew was just
as friendly as she was. They were really into having a
good time.

We lit a fire, the men set up a few logs.
Daphne's kids were in their late teens to early 20's.
They had a speaker port for the iPhone and played
music. Granted, we didn't know most of the songs, but
when they asked where we were from and we said
Atlanta, they turned up for us. They were taking pics
with Sade. They recognized her as more of a
personality than an actress.

It was so amazing! We made s'mores, drank
wine and nibbled on fruit. It was just good, wholesome
fun. In my head, I'm thinking, *this is kinda cute or
whatever.* I still wasn't ready to let loose. I could tell
British wasn't either. It was something we hadn't
really experienced before. For some reason, it was
hard to trust how welcoming these strangers were.

Then the food came out from one of their villas.
Their chefs hauled a tub full of hot dogs and sausages
out to the shore. They set up a little table for the food
and condiments. Paris danced on this sexy guy with
blonde hair, we found out later his name was Adler.
Curls dangled just past his shoulders. When he swept it
up in one of those effortless buns, he blew us all away.
He was gorgeous. I was instantly glad that she had her
own room, just in case he ended up back there. Paris
was a little chunky, but Adler was hugging all of her
curves.

It was actually just the kind of no fuss atmosphere we needed. By the time our new English friends got the clambake going, me and all my Divas had let loose. We were singing, drinking, dancing, drinking, eating and drinking.

In the distance coming down one of the trails, we could see candles. Daphne's kids brought out trays with mini cupcakes on them. Each cupcake had a number one candle on it, they were singing and we joined right in.

"Awwww!!" Daphne was in tears before the cupcakes made it to her. She kissed her children and her husband. "You guys mean so much to me. I love you all for making this trip across the pond with me. A year ago today, I didn't think I was going to live. I was in a horrible accident and almost lost my life. Lying there in the hospital bed I had nothing but time to think about my life and talk to the Lord. I thought about my wonderful husband, George, whose face was the first one I saw when I woke up from my coma, and our four children who we have raised over the last 25 years."

"I thought to myself, that I was by no means ready to die. But if the Lord saw fit to take me, I had already experienced more love and laughter than most people even dream. There were still things I wanted to do, goals I had to set aside to raise our kids. One of those goals was to finish college. I dropped out when I got pregnant with Margo and never went back. So, today, I announce to everyone, that I have enrolled in university to begin in the fall!" Daphne gave a fist pump and the crowd cheered. We cheered her on as well.

"I'm so excited! Me and George have made a pact that this is the first of our annual trips. Each year, we are going to a new place we have never been before. My dream is to travel and see the world! And eat lots and lots of food!" We all laughed. "To all of you here, whatever your heart desires, do it! Don't give up on anything! On love…on laughter…on your dreams…You never know when the time will come that you are no longer able to. I'm going to find a reason to smile, even on my worst days because that is one more day I almost didn't have."

"Daphne, you're so longwinded, the candles blew out, Dear," her husband said. Everybody laughed. The music came back on and we got back to it!

Daphne's husband grabbed Kennedi's hand and danced with her. He recognized her from the posters his oldest son used to put on the walls in his room. Daphne's crew went crazy when they first saw Kennedi. They took pictures with her and even played some of her songs.

Kennedi kept thinking about Daphne saying not giving up on your dreams. It was as if Daphne was speaking directly to Kennedi. Dancing barefoot in the sand under the moonlight, Kennedi was thinking about her future, about feeling fulfilled. Through the years she has struggled to maintain an identity, let me tell you about it.

Kennedi, the beautiful Kennedi, looked like an angel and sounded like one, too. Her ass is so damn talented and honey that caramel skin is flawless. Unlike British who sought after men in the music industry, Kennedi was a money maker. She performed at talent shows for years until the right person with the right connections heard her and was able to get her in front of record label execs.

The label agreed and put her out as their premier female solo act. When it was all said and done, the kid was a hit. Throughout the 90's, Kennedi burned up the charts. She easily had almost two dozen top ten hits, was featured on TV shows, and even a movie or two. All the teenage girls wanted to be Kennedi. The influence she had on the country was amazing. Hell, I even wanted to be like Kennedi at one point.

Her energy was infectious, which is what people liked about her. To meet Kennedi was to love her. Life as a musician was hard, especially back in the day traveling from city to city, spending very little if at any time at home with family. She began to seek other opportunities. It was on one of those acting gigs that she met Ty Woodley. Before I go any further, let me just say, Ty is one of the finest men you will ever come across. Ever! He was the 1990's type of fine, light-skinned, dark brown curly hair with hints of natural blonde, slender build with hazel eyes.

They met on a set, really casual. Their interaction was cool, but Kennedi was more concerned with learning her lines than trying to mack some little, wanna-be, film director. A few years later, homeboy had cut off that curly carrot top and sported a 3 p.m. shadow. The definition he gained in those muscles only helped his case. This time when they ran into each other at a music awards show, she was ready to listen to anything he had to say.

During that time, he was busy adding to his portfolio. He was able to successfully produce and direct films in virtually every genre. His style was not cookie cutter or predictable. You could not see one of his movies and think, *This is a Ty Woodley film.* The women swooned over him and his cast mates loved his take charge attitude, which won him popularity in Hollywood. Ty slowly crept over into the white side of directing.

"How's my beautiful girl?" He always greeted her that way, or called her his angel. He hugged and kissed her, making her really feel loved. Her heart always jumped when she saw him. Their relationship flourished. Kennedi wanted to stay in music after dabbling in a few other things; she learned that music truly was her passion.

She took a well-deserved break to rejuvenate herself and jumpstart her career with a hot, fresh sound. Plus, you know how it is when you get into a new relationship and you want to just be with your boo all the time. You forget about everything and everybody else. That's the space Kennedi was in.

Ty scooped her up and told her she could take her time. Ty grew up in a house with both parents, where his mother took care of the three kids and his father brought home the bread. There was a lot of love and support in the home. Growing up, he wanted to be able to provide for his wife and kids the same way his father had.

Kennedi was totally smitten with the thought of having someone take care of her. She was raised with her mom and sister around the corner from a slew of aunts, uncles and cousins. Kennedi was halfway supporting the whole block. She worked hard for her money, but her family just saw her as a cash cow.

Hearing that Ty wanted to take care of her was a welcomed relief. She spent her time back and forth between L.A. and Atlanta. She went with Ty to auditions, script readings and set scouting. He wouldn't roll out of bed for less than $5 million. With that much security, Kennedi took longer and longer to come back onto the music scene.

News of their engagement hit, making them the "it" couple. They made all kinds of couple of the year spreads in magazines and blogs. She saw them being a power couple; he was quickly becoming the most well-known black film director and her vocal pipes would land her at the top of the charts with any single.

Kennedi was ready to get back into the studio. She was still wildly popular in the eyes of the public, but she missed the energy around rehearsing, performing, bringing out new singles and getting dolled up. There was something about the air when a crowd of tens of thousands of fans were chanting her name.

Back in the 90's when she got started, nobody knew what the internet was. Fast forward about ten years. Myspace was extinct, Facebook was all the rage and people were tweeting. Fans could see her without her having to travel through tiny towns hitting up small clubs on the chitlin' circuit. She could be more selective and perform only huge concerts in big arenas.

"But I *want* to sing!" was always her response. She wasn't afraid of hard work. That was one of the reasons he chose her. Even though he was holding it down, he wanted to be sure that his woman wasn't lazy. Ty had to know his lady could jump in there and work if she had to.

Ty told her to focus on the wedding. This is around the time I met her. Paris brought her into the fold after doing her hair a few times and liking her down to earth vibe. The Divas were starting to come together, honey!

The invite list of their anticipated nuptials was going to be a who's who of Hollywood royalty. People were clamoring to get invited and trying to invite themselves. Security had to be beefed up to keep unwanted people with their fucked up energy out of the room. Kennedi dreamt up this fantastical wedding unlike anything she had ever seen.

She requested that all of her guests wear white. The wording on the invitation was something along the lines of letting guests know if they didn't wear white, they would not be allowed inside. At first, people thought it was a cute suggestion, then guests began asking them if they were serious and word spread quickly that they were. Magazines even got word of it and ran the story.

The ceremony and reception rooms at first seemed almost sterile. White chairs, white tile floors created just for the event, along with white ceiling décor. There were shimmery accents all around, but the pop of color was the floral arrangements. Lavender hydrangeas, plum roses and decadent midnight orchids infused the room with shades of purple in ways that had never been seen before. The bride's dress was a gorgeous soft pink, complimented by the flowers of course, to stand out amongst the crowd. The guests gasped when she walked in the room.

It was the perfect day. The only thing that could possibly ruin it was Ty smashing her in the face with the cake. She threatened his ass about messing up her thousand dollar beat and it never happened.

Work quickly brought them back to Atlanta. Ty went to work and Kennedi went with him. She quickly grew bored of set life. Spending all day and night in a trailer or outside on location watching them rehearse the same scene repeatedly was incredibly tedious. If one of the actors did not show up, or was late, Kennedi eagerly jumped in to read their lines. She began talking about how watching him live out his dreams and making career moves made her miss the studio. He shushed her, like a she was a child and tasked her with finding a house for them to buy.

By their one year anniversary, Kennedi was truly a kept woman…bored and unfulfilled. She had all the bags and shoes in the world and was not happy.

She hated that in order to feel good about herself, she had to reach back to memories of her glory days. She felt like she wasn't doing anything with her life. Some days, she did not even get out of her pajamas. Kennedi knew there had to be more to life than just existing. Hanging out with friends just wasn't cutting it anymore.

"Bae, I've been working on some new lyrics," Kennedi said to Ty. Her excitement almost disgusted him.

"How many times do I have to tell you, I got this! You don't need to do that work shit anymore. You are my *wife* now! I'll take care of you." His words were forceful and his tone was harsh.

After spending a decade on the world's stages, seeing America the way most only dream and filling up passports within a matter of months, there were not many things that could light her fire the way singing could. It gave her such a high that either she had to get back in it or find something equally as thrilling. She figured that showing Ty a good time by giving him something he really wanted, would open him up to be more receptive to her needs.

She got dressed, went to get a mani/pedi, then drove her Mercedes Maybach to a restaurant. It was a spot that was known for its drinks, but off the beaten path so there wouldn't be a lot of people there which is just what she needed. Kennedi walked right up to the bar and plopped down in a chair.

"Welcome in today ma'am, what'll ya have?" the bartender asked.

"Lemme get a daiquiri."

"One daiquiri, coming up," she laughed. When she turned around, Kennedi noticed her butt hanging out of the jean shorts she wore.

"Nice ass."

"Excuse me?" The bartender genuinely couldn't make out what she said.

"Nothing," Kennedi laughed. She was used to looking at women. She and Ty looked at chicks, checking them out and that was about as far as it went. They had been to a strip club or two together. Kennedi wasn't offended by her husband's remarks. She knew she was not the first woman he had ever been with and it showed her what he liked, what he was into.

They toyed with the idea of bringing another woman into their bed for kicks. Ty tried to see if he could get his wife to go along with it. It never went beyond being a fantasy.

"Here is your drink," the bartender put a napkin down in front of Kennedi. As she sat the glass down, she brushed Kennedi's hand. Kennedi looked her right in the face, but she didn't look up. Kennedi downed the daiquiri quickly.

"Ma'am," Kennedi waved to get her attention. She was busy fixing other drinks. "Ma'am!"

"Yes, what else can I get you, Doll?"

"Your name."

"Rachel," she laughed.

"Ok, Ms. Rachel, I will have a Sex on the Beach."

"Hmmmm, Sex on the Beach? Nice choice. I had sex on the beach once, well a few times, but one time was the best." Rachel leaned closer to the bar and lowered her voice. "It was broad day light and my boyfriend and I were chillin' on the beach in Hawaii. We rented two chairs and a big beach umbrella. When the sun started to set, he took the umbrella and laid it kinda on its side, then pulled me on top of him on his chair. I wrapped myself in a big beach towel, pulled my thong to the side and put him inside me. I leaned forward and rode him real slow. It was so wild because, there were people walking past, but it looked like I was just laying there. Well, sort of. I'm sure somebody knew what was going on, but nobody said anything." Rachel put the drink cup down on the napkin.

Kennedi twisted around in her bar chair. She easily got a vivid visual of Rachel's ass barely moving under a big beach towel. She visualized Rachel's legs covered in sand, trying to stifle the sounds of satisfying sex. Kennedi got excited, but knew Ty would like it even more.

"Wow," Kennedi said when Rachel walked back over. "That sounds like fun. I sure need some of that. I haven't had sex in months." Lies! Of course Kennedi was having sex. She was having no children in the house, they could do whatever they wanted in whatever room they wanted sex.

"Months?" Rachel spoke like she didn't believe.

"Months."

"Why do you think that is?"

"I don't know," Kennedi shrugged her shoulders.

"Do you think there's somebody else?"

"Oh, I'm sure it is."

"What?" Rachel's eyes got really big thinking she was about to get some juicy tea.

"Yep. I met that ho'!" Kennedi took her drink to the head.

"No, ma'am!" Rachel stopped moving and stared at Kennedi. "He would cheat on you? Kennedi?"

"Yep, with his job...and I let him!" They both fell out laughing. "Hit me with a Blue Muthafucka."

"Now, if I give you this third drink, after the last two, I can't let you go home alone. That may be dangerous. You'll be too slizurred up to drive."

"I'll uber."

"No, no, no," Rachel insisted. "I need to know you made it home...safely."

When Ty walked in the house a couple hours later, he found Kennedi and Rachel sharing wine, laughing butt naked on the chase portion of the couch.

"Perfect timing, Babe!" His mouth flew open. His feet were frozen. He didn't know whether to run and jump between them, stand and watch or kick the damn girl out. Let's be honest, kicking the girl out probably never crossed his mind. "C'mon over," Kennedi placed her wine glass down then began sucking on Rachel's tit.

"Now this is what I'm talking about!" Ty laughed and stumbled forward. By the time he reached them, Kennedi was coursing her tongue from Rachel's nipple down to her belly button. Rachel giggled and guided Kennedi's head down lower. Ty approached the ladies and Rachel unbuttoned his pants and let them fall to the floor. Rachel hungrily put him in her mouth, while Kennedi massaged Rachel with hers. Kennedi wanted the excitement of the moment to be more for Ty than herself and she positioned Ty behind Rachel doggy style so she could be pleased orally. That first experience was magical for them all.

The next morning, Ty asked his wife why she abruptly decided to change her mind. Kennedi expressed just how bored she was and she knew it was a desire of his. She had no work, no children, nothing to occupy her time other than shopping and spending money. With Atlanta shopping, walking around the same stores was lame. New items didn't come in that often.

In reality, Kennedi knew if she gave him something he wanted, he would return the favor. So far, Ty was not giving her any support to go back to singing. She wanted him to have her back.

He had so much fun with Rachel, he wanted to do it again. Kennedi obliged because it was such a deviation from the norm, she had a blast with it too. She wanted his ass to keep having fun, so when she told him it was studio time, he would not have any issue. The unexpected bonus was how it ramped up the sex between just the two of them. Their passion reached a new high, there was now even more excitement in the bedroom.

"Rachel, did you wear that dress to make it easier for me?" Ty asked licking his lips.

"C'mon over here," Rachel answered grabbing his head and pushing him down to his knees. She easily became very comfortable with the couple. It was on and poppin' from that point.

Kennedi went back to the spot to get Rachel yet again. This time, Kennedi cut to the chase and told her to have her ass at the house after work. Kennedi answered the door, grabbing Rachel's hand and pulling her quickly into the house. Kennedi closed the door, pushed Rachel up against it, grabbed her face and kissed her passionately. The juices were already flowing.

"Damn, Rachel, you look nice!" Ty noted from where he sat. Kennedi looked at him thinking that he hadn't said that to her in a minute! She wanted a compliment, too. But she didn't want to ruin the mood.

Kennedi escorted Rachel to a guest bedroom with a shower, helped her get undressed and let her shower. When Rachel came out, Kennedi was in between Ty's legs, sprawled wide open giving him head on the bed. Rachel, still damp, walked right over to the bed and joined in the fun. When it was over, Kennedi left the room and came back with a wad of cash.

"How much?" she asked. Rachel was still coming down from her nut.

"Huh?"

"What's your price for sleeping with us?" Kennedi could not have Rachel confused, thinking she was their girlfriend. Being a girlfriend came with perks, especially with a couple who was that well connected. She would go on trips, get gifts and go to private, invite only events. Kennedi was not having any of that. Rachel needed to know exactly what purpose she served, she was not a friend, she was a fuck.

"I don't have a price," Rachel said almost offended.

"Here's two grand." Kennedi peeled 20 hundred dollar bills and placed them on top of Rachel's clothes.

"I didn't do this for the money."

"I bet," Kennedi laughed. "Thank you." Kennedi laid down next to Ty and kissed his chest. Rachel flung the covers back, jumped out of bed grabbing her clothes. She angrily marched out of the room, slamming the front door a minute later. She didn't even stop to put on her clothes.

"What was that for?" Ty asked. He was mad that his wife just ran away the side booty that *she* brought in the house in the first place!

"She needs to know her place. This is just for fun, this is not a relationship. Rachel ain't one of the homies."

"Now, who are we going to fuck? You just ran her off!"

"We'll find somebody. That won't be hard."

Kennedi showed him that she was willing to do whatever to please him, now it was his turn to return the favor. She wrote a song and told him she wanted him to hear it. As she sang, he acted excited at first, then told her she was wasting her time.

"Look, Bae, you've been gone so long, singing just isn't your scene anymore!"

"Damn, I'm not 50! It's only been a few years."

"And in those years, more artists have come out. Your fans are on to the next. The streets ain't loyal, Bae! You need to just settle into being a wife."

"*You* give me a hookup!"

"How? C'mon Bae, I'm in the film industry, Kennedi, not music."

"Movies have scenes with a sexy lounge singer crooning under dim lights or wedding scenes when the bride is walking down the aisle." She pushed up on him from behind, wrapping her arms around his chiseled stomach. "Let me be the sultry singer in a dark, sexy club singing my hot, new shit and by the time the movie comes out, I could have an album ready to go!" She looked at him excitedly.

"Nah, Bae, I think you should leave it alone." Ty completely brushed her off. Again.

She decided to go against him and go to a studio anyway. She only had one song, far from an album, but recording was a drug that she could not deny. It pulled at her the way nothing else did. It was easy for her to book a session having that kind of history behind her. Producers would jump at a chance to help her make a comeback.

Kennedi got so carried away that she spent hours in the lab. She completely lost track of time. When she finally looked at her phone, she saw Ty had called and texted several times. He wasn't used to not being able to get ahold of his wife. He was between being worried something happened to her and upset thinking that she was ignoring him. As she read the texts, the phone rang again.

"Hello!"

"Hey, Bae, I…" She answered calmly.

"Don't hey Bae me! Why weren't you answering your phone?"

"I stopped by the studio and Flex was here. We just choppin' it up."

"Come home now! I don't want you up there!"

"You buggin' right now, for real!"

"Now, I told you I don't want you up there. Ain't shit up in the studio for you. There's no reason for you to be there!"

"Bae, I'll be home soon."

"I ain't playing games with your ass. Come on now, Kennedi!"

"Quit being so dramatic. I'll be home in a little bit."

"I'm on my way!" Kennedi took the phone away from her face and saw the time flashing. *This fool hung up on me.* She didn't want to bring that kind of drama to the studio and Ty was being unreasonably difficult. This kind of behavior was unlike him.

Racing home, Kennedi knew they needed to have a come to Jesus conversation. She had no intentions of living her life in his shadow. Her dream was to find a husband who she could build with, not watch him build. She wanted to be doing boss shit in her industry, while he did boss shit in his. You know, be better together. She thought she found that in Ty. She was already moving and shaking in the music industry and he was turning heads with his movies. The public loved them together, there was nothing else to be done but be the power couple that everybody saw them as being.

Kennedi felt in her heart like she was being stifled. He didn't want her to build anything. Instead, he was killing off any passion she had. There was something burning to get off of her chest. The time was now.

"Ty, we need to talk." She walked into the living room where he was reading through scripts. I'm tired of this shit. I am not the type of woman who wants to be kept. I enjoy you taking care of me, but doing what I love doesn't feel like work. It gives me pride and satisfaction seeing my dreams come to life. It helps me feel alive!" She was proud of the speech she rehearsed over and over.

"No wife of mine is working! Feel alive another way."

"Stop being so…so…so damn controlling. You said I could take my time with my career. Shit! I had no plans of retiring myself before 30!"

"Did you ever think about the sense of pride it gives me to take care of you?"

"Ty, don't you get it? It's about being constructive with my time, doing something I enjoy doing.

"Face it Bae, I make way more money than you ever could."

Kennedi's eyes filled with tears. She scooped up her car keys and ran out to her car. She left so fast, she left her phone and he knew there would be no way of reaching her. He wouldn't know where she was or what she was doing, he would just have to wait on her to come back.

The sun was rising when she came back home. She was gone almost a full twelve hours. She really needed to clear her head and get away from him. Kennedi wanted to see if she was being unrealistic or not. After replaying several of the conversations in her head, nothing led her to believe that she was being unrealistic.

She decided it was time to have a baby. She wanted to start trying immediately. Ty was spending more time away on set. His last two films were blockbusters! Ty was becoming so busy that his agent had to drop his other clients. Going from speaking engagements to movies to endorsement spots, Ty had arrived!

They made the best of the time when he was home. He was tired from basically living on set, spending 12 to 16 hour days filming. Kennedi still pounced on him and they fucked like rabbits until he had to leave again. If he made quick trips for auditions or premiers, she accompanied him.

Kennedi felt overwhelmed. She didn't know anybody who was *trying* to have a baby and couldn't. Starting a family was something they both grew to desperate want. She wouldn't feel like a woman unless she could give her husband a child.

She took a long, hot shower. The enormity of trying completely stressed her out. She wanted to wash her cares right down the drain. The bathroom mirror was completely covered in steam. That didn't stop her from singing to an imaginary audience. Wrapped in a soft, terry cloth towel, she picked up her brush and sang her heart out. Kennedi swiped the mirror and looked at herself as she sang her heart out. She couldn't even recognize herself looking through a wall of tears. She was hurting so desperately and wanted the tide to turn in her life.

Through it all, she maintained that she wanted to hop back in the studio. But not getting pregnant was weighing heavily on her mind. Kennedi went to the doctor to get checked out and see what she could do naturally to conceive.

Ty suggested that they find a girl to fuck. He told her it would ease her mind. They started the night at a strip club. It had been a while since the two of them had done anything fun. Kennedi planned on enjoying the night with her husband. Once they arrived, they were immediately escorted to a VIP area.

Before they could even get seated, a girl was checking on them to get their drinks ordered. Four girls crowded the area and began practically fighting their way into the booth. They knew with celebrities like Kennedi and Ty, some real money was going to be spent.

The couple took it all in, the vibe was great and the energy was high. The building was practically shaking from the low, hard-hitting bass blasting out of the speakers. Girls were giving lap dances, others were walking around trying to find willing patrons. Stacks and British came over, hugged and said hi. They all shot the shit for a few songs, then British and Stacks headed back to their booth.

"Look at her," Ty said into his wife's ear. He nodded to a girl with a hot pink bikini bottom and beautiful round breasts. Kennedi had been thinking about her.

"Mmmm," Kennedi could barely hear Ty. He didn't mean for her to hear, but she was in tune with her man. "I want her," he nodded to the stage. There was a girl in a blue one piece. Her outfit looked like strings with small patches over the nipples and vagina. She moved so slowly, it was almost painful to watch, but it was so seductive. Ty couldn't take his eyes off of her. Her hair was long and wavy with a chunk of blue in the bang. She had a tattoo of flowers that wrapped from under one breast around to the top of her ass crack.

"Make some change! Make some change!" The DJ blasted overhead. "Sapphire comin' to da stage and y'all know how she do! I want e'erybody in the building to come show muh girl some love! Leggo!"

Without warning, Sapphire fell into a split as soon as the beat dropped. The DJ really liked her, so he gave her one of the hottest songs in the game. She bounced up and down effortlessly while rolling her torso at the same time. One of the other dancers walked onto the stage with a chair, opened it, then sat down in it.

"Oh shit! Y'all know it's about to go down. When Sapphire brang out a chair, ya know she 'bout to get down to bidness! C'mon with dem ones!" The DJ blasted.

As Sapphire did the stripper stroll around the girl on the chair, more strippers and patrons crowded around the stage. Ty sat up on the couch to make sure he didn't miss anything. Sapphire climbed up the pole on stage, swung her legs up over her head and started pussy popping in a hand stand, while holding on to the pole! Instead of just coming back down, she flipped her whole body and landed in the lap of the girl on the chair. The place went bananas! While dollars rained on the stage, the girl slapped Sapphire's ass and it wobbled as if it sounded like thunder rolling.

By the time she finished her routine, the stage was completely covered in money. You couldn't even see the stage. The bouncers brought her big black trash bags and a broom to get it all. She walked away with three bags.

"Her." Ty said. Kennedi told the girl who was grinding on her to go get Sapphire. When Sapphire came out, she was in leggings a cute top, totally not work appropriate. Sapphire explained that she had only planned to work one set that night. She was past the point of giving lap dances, unless they were at private parties.

Kennedi thought that was interesting, but she could easily see how. Sapphire made more money in her three or four song set than most of the girls made all night. Kennedi told her to meet them at a hotel and

Sapphire agreed. Even though Ty and Kennedi had been tipping the girls for the last hour, he gave them all three hundreds as he grabbed Kennedi's hand and they left.

Once in the room, Ty ordered champagne and strawberries from room service. Kennedi walked Sapphire to the bathroom where the glass shower was. They dropped their clothes on the marble floor and hopped in. He sat there and watched them fondle each other and bathe. It was a beautiful sight. Ty was so excited, he couldn't wait to stick his piece inside of Sapphire.

"I can't wait to make that ass clap," Ty said to Sapphire when they stepped out. She was still dripping wet, he slowly rubbed his hand down the curve of her hips. She blushed and Kennedi put her hand on his back. The three of them got busy right there in the bathroom. The room service arrived after round one. They laid in the bed feeding each other and drinking the champagne. Ty slipped under the covers and began eating Sapphire out. Round two.

What Kennedi began to notice over time, between threesomes with strippers or women they came across in public, was her husband had stopped being attracted to her sexually. In her mind it was because she could not bear him any children and he felt like she wasn't really a woman.

He got off on her letting him have sex with other women. Even though it was more for his enjoyment than hers, the agreement was that they had to do it together. Initially, Kennedi was into it. She loved having threesomes. They turned her on as much as they did Ty. Seeing that Ty preferred to have sex together with other women took some of the thrill away from her. She wasn't enough for him anymore. He barely looked at her and when he did, she had to work to excite him.

He complimented the other women, he salivated over them, he fantasized about them when he was with Kennedi. When they had sex, he fucked Kennedi while talking about past ménages they had, claiming that he was trying to turn her on more. It was all too much. She continued having threesomes to please him.

Kennedi started to feel uncomfortable about it. When other girls were in the room, he forgot about her. It seemed like she was only there so she couldn't come back and say he had done it without her.

She told him that she did not want to do them anymore. Ty looked at her like she had three heads. He came at her with some bullshit.

"Bae," Ty started, "that kind of fantasy will help relieve some of the stress you deal with on a regular basis. You need a break from reality. All you worry about is trying to get pregnant and get in the studio, neither of which is working for you."

"I am the one who initiated this. I'm telling you I don't want to do that anymore. That should be good enough for you."

"You don't mean it."

"I absolutely do."

"Would you feel more comfortable if we had a steady girl? I'll even let you choose." He was proud that in his mind, he had come up with a solution. Kennedi was insulted that he said he would *let* her choose.

"I need a career. I need that release."

"You release every time we fuck somebody," he laughed hard, clearly amusing himself. Kennedi stared at him.

"I have been doing this for years to make you happy. I have done whatever you needed or wanted me to do. You are not supporting the *one* thing that I ask of you to make me happy."

"Nobody wants to hear your washed up ass trying to hop on a mic. You are a has been...a *Where Are They Now* special."

"It's not all about me being in the studio. I want to find talent. I can be a manager. I can write songs, there are so many areas of the music industry."

"You better find fulfillment picking out some drapes because the only jobs you are going to have are wife and mother."

"I...AM...NOT...A...MOTHER!" she yelled in frustration.

"Let's make it happen, Kennedi. We have all the money in the world, it shouldn't be a problem. We can get a surrogate or do that in vitro shit."

"I don't want a damn surrogate."

"Make an appointment for in vitro. Let's get this show on the road!"

Kennedi made the appointment and they spoke to the doctor. For the mere...absurd...cost of $20,000 they could try in vitro. The doctor explained the whole process and they were excited to give it a try.

It didn't work. They tried again. Kennedi's heart was still filled with tremendous hope and promise. She was excited that modern technology would allow her to get to this point. She was going to be a mother after all. She was very nervous about it, but told The Divas.

We were all crunk about it too. We went out for a celebratory dinner to help lift her spirits. We knew how much it meant to Kennedi to have mini Kennedi's and mini Ty's. She was a good person, with a good heart. We encouraged her the best way we could.

The second attempt failed. So did the third. Kennedi was starting to swirl deeper and deeper into disappointment. The doctor said there seemed to be nothing wrong with either of them, it just wasn't happening naturally and the in vitro wasn't sticking. She was starting to feel her life spiral in the wrong direction.

She got the call about the last in vitro try as she was getting ready to meet Ty at a premier. The call could not have come at a worse time. Kennedi knew she couldn't not show up for the premier. People expected her to be on the red carpet. She finished getting ready and got into the car service.

Kennedi was so beside herself, she couldn't stop the tears from falling. She was able to catch them fast and thank God for waterproof mascara, but seeing herself try and fail to become pregnant over and over was becoming too much. As they rounded the corner for the red carpet, she dabbed her eyes again. She looked up at the roof of the car, blinking the tears back so she could refresh her face. "Time to put this mask back on, Kennedi. You have to be a happy, supportive wife tonight. Your life is together. You have it all. Other people would kill to be where you are," she said to hype herself up.

She made it up in her mind that she would show Ty that she was about her business. What hurt was how he always instantly went to degrading her, never supporting her dreams. She complimented him on his films and great directing ability, practiced scenes for him, went to auditions and award shows. She was there for him, yet he did not offer the same support. She knew he was afraid that she would come back into the spotlight and be bigger than he was. She just didn't have the balls to tell him that.

Sadly, she realized that the only thing that really validated her was the public. She had a near flawless body, but she worked out relentlessly, and ate healthy foods. She compared herself to the images of other singers and actors even though she knew in their day to day lives, they didn't even look the same as they did on film and in pictures. Everything was smoke and mirrors.

Kennedi started telling Ty she was hanging with The Divas, but instead, she was booking studio time. Thinking about the career she wanted to have, she wrote a pop club banger. She studied the hot songs that were out, then infused a little of that old Kennedi flavor. She was good to go! Being a pro, my girl got it down in a few sessions. Interested to see if she could conjure up some of the old buzz, she took the single to radio stations in Atlanta and asked them to add it to their rotation. In less than seven days, her single was in the top three songs requested on every station.

Ty got word that his wife had a new, hot single on the airwaves. People were calling and texting him saying they were glad she was back. Angry, he ran to the stations to get the DJ's to take it out of their rotation. Cold hard cash makes it easy for people to change their minds. He paid the DJ's not to play it.

Sade was the one who heard Ty was paying the stations off. Sade called Kennedi to let her know, friend to friend, that's what the streets were saying. Sadly, one of the DJ's leaked the info to the blogs, which got national spotlight and the story took off. *Ty Revels Pays Atlanta Radio Stations Not To Play His Wife Kennedi's New Single!*

The press had a field day with it. Neither Kennedi nor Ty responded to the article. Kennedi tweeted a thank you to the public for still believing in her.

Coming home from a good workout, Kennedi was surprised to see Ty sitting in the living room. He sat there with a tumbler glass, no ice just cognac. It was the middle of the day.

"Hey, Bae."

"See how you got me out here looking in these streets?"

"What 'chu mean?"

"I told you not to go to the studio. I told you to leave that music shit alone. But you…had to go do what you wanted anyway. I'm big enough for the both of us!"

"Ty, we have been trying to conceive for four years. Three naturally and one with in vitro. That shit is wearing me out." She walked closer and saw him sitting in front of her notebook full of lyrics. "What are you doing with that?"

"This…bullshit that nobody wants to hear? I'm going to get rid of it."

"What is your problem?!" The tears fell easily. She was a walking emotional basket case.

"I'm just taking out the trash." Ty lit the pages in the book with a lighter. Kennedi ran over to him scrambling to snatch it away. He jumped up with his back to her moving swiftly to keep her from getting it until the pages were burned too badly.

"Fuck you, Ty! Fuck you!" she shouted as he laughed and walked away.

Reeling from the fact that one of the DJ's took the story to a blog, Ty was livid and unrelenting. He saw how positive the public's outcry was about his wife having new music. His punk ass didn't care. Kennedi realized just how afraid he was that her career would eclipse his. What she thought was only a need to be able to provide for his family and show his father that he could, was really a lack of confidence bordering on jealousy. It was totally unfounded because the fickle public loved him and thought he was talented as well.

Now, there was a refreshed interest in Kennedi. She was able to land a lucrative endorsement deal with a major national makeup powerhouse, as well as be featured on the covers of magazines.

Not really being into the whole Kennedi craze, Ty went behind Kennedi's back and began seeing Sapphire. They were sleeping together on a regular basis, which was easy to do with his hectic acting schedule and her equally as hectic 'I don't give a fuck' attitude. With Kennedi's deeply rooted feelings of alienation, she wasn't exactly trying to keep tabs on him. She was too busy sneaking back into the studio to record another hit.

Drastically, she saw a lawyer and had divorce papers drawn up. She had no intention on getting a divorce, she wanted to scare him straight. She had spent too many years being miserable living under him. She was not his property and had to reclaim her life before she looked back and 20 years had passed her by in a dark haze.

Ty did not give her the reaction she wanted. When she presented him with the papers, this fool moved out of the house! If she wanted a divorce, he was going to give her one. He took Sapphire on a widely publicized trip, making sure they both took pictures practically every hour to post. Ty made sure that pictures of the two of them were seen everywhere. Kennedi was devastated. She was not worried about the lifestyle or the money she had grown accustomed to since he became a top film dynamo, she wanted her husband back. She missed their love and their friendship.

Maybe the trip Ty went on was a cry for help. He could have been trying to use that as a scare tactic for Kennedi to come back to him. She was hurt, but somewhat relieved. It felt good not to have to tip toe around to do what she felt she was born to do. For the first time in years, she was invited to the music awards and was even asked to present.

Her confidence was rekindled. Ty had her feeling like nobody was checking for her. He never gave her compliments, instead he relished on the girls they slept with. He got so free with it that they could be just walking in the store and he'd walk up to a complete stranger and tell her how pretty she was. Kennedi would have to contain her feelings, like it didn't bother her. She didn't want the other women to see her insecurities. She was so sweet and hated the thought of confrontation to the point that she barely said anything about it.

Kennedi was photographed with another presenter, an NBA MVP. He was fresh on the heels of a divorce and it looked like Kennedi was next in his sights. Especially after what had just gone down with Ty parading his trick around. The blogs went crazy. The MVP publicly went on his social media and refuted the rumors.

He posted the pic all of the blogs posted side by side with the real pic. In the real pic, there were three other female presenters on his other side. As it turned out, the paparazzi who took the pic was clearly trying to get some cake from it, because he cut the other women out of it. The MVP commented under the picture, "We were all presenters. I am a fan of the beautiful, talented Kennedi. We are in no way associated beyond the stage of this award ceremony." The statement was obviously prepared by his team, but he stood behind it.

Kennedi put what little energy she had left into rebuilding her music career. She focused on a new image and the right single to throw into the music scene. In three months, Kennedi got a dope stylist, totally revamped her image from hair styles on down, gave herself a refreshed signature sound and started putting feelers out with a demo.

It was a very exciting time for her. Kennedi used her connections to get blog press, music execs and radio personalities to come through. The Divas were so proud of her and encouraged her by helping to plan a showcase. She scheduled the event only two weeks out. There was a lot to be done in a short amount of time. Kennedi was up for the challenge. She wanted to be the center of attention that night, then the talk of the music industry the next day.

The event was going off without a hitch. Influential people were arriving, the drinks were flowing, the butler passed hors d'oeuvres were also a hit. The Divas were handling things. We were checking on everyone to make sure they were straight, staying on top of the chef and bartenders to keep the guests from waiting, even making sure everyone had a goodie bag in their hand as they walked out.

The only missing piece was Ty. Kennedi tried to shield her hurt, but those who knew her could see that she was in pain. Her heart ached for her husband. He missed so much!

She was doing the very thing he told her she could not do, yet, she wished to only share it with him. Those feelings of abandonment hit her the hardest when she was in bed alone. A California king sized bed is exceptionally cold and lonely when you get used to sharing it with someone. She would hug her pillow and cry. Her muffled cries couldn't be heard by anyone. She was alone in 12,000 square feet of space.

She teetered between sadness and anger. Angry that he left her for a fucking stripper. Angry that they couldn't start a family. Angry that he ran right out and got with one of the girls they had been with, so she figured they had been fucking the whole time. She was upset that he found her as an artist, a working woman, then did everything in his power to diminish her to a point where she barely believed in herself.

There was a shift in her thinking. She had to prove to him, and more importantly herself not to give up and to go after your heart. British found her crying in the back room where she was getting ready. So British gave Kennedi a pep talk before it was time to roll.

"You got this! Ok Mama? You know you are a star. Everybody here knows you are a star. We all got ya back! We wanna see Kennedi blow this bitch down! You hear me? Now you go rock this shit like you were born to do! I dropped some coins on a new pair of shoes for this damn singing thing, so you better tear this shit up! Wipe these damn tears, its show time bitch!" They laughed.

The curtains opened on the small stage in the intimate venue. Ty was standing in the middle. He sucked the air out of the room. Literally! Everybody either gasped, or their mouths flew wide open. Kennedi went from shock to happiness to being pissed off in one second. He could see the look on her face, as could everybody else. He was determined to ruin her big night. Her eyes brimmed with tears in frustration. The Divas were closing in on him. British jumped on the stage and was ready to attempt to physically get 'bout it' if necessary.

"Kennedi," he spoke. The crowd's attention turned to her. Before any words flew out of her mouth he shouted, "Let me talk. Let me talk. I'm sorry, I didn't believe in you. For many selfish reasons, I wanted to keep you home, barefoot and pregnant," he laughed expecting everybody else to. No one was amused.

"These months away from you were exciting," he continued and the first tears fell from Kennedi's eyes. British tried to take the mic away from him. "That was at first. I realized that I am nothing without you. My life is empty. I am miserable. Whatever it is you want...or don't...we can work it out. I want to be the reason you smile. Will you continue being my wife?" Ty asked dropping down on one knee. The room erupted! The crowd was cheering, clapping and screaming.

The rest of the night was perfect. She did her thing on the stage and the feedback was positive. For the first time in over four months, Kennedi and Ty had a late dinner together. He did exactly what he said during his speech, supported and encouraged her.

They began working on her music together. He was between films and knew Kennedi would appreciate him helping her pick beats and write lyrics. He scheduled studio sessions, and meetings with record execs. What started out as Kennedi's come back turned into Ty trying to convince her to start back trying to have kids. She was in a place where she could easily see herself going back down the path where they were before.

He gave her an ultimatum…their marriage or her career. That was a decision Kennedi felt she should not have had to make.

"You selfish muthafucka! And that's not a word throw around. This shit ain't cool! This is not what I signed up for. I love the fact that you are a man and you want to take care of your woman, but if you love me the way you say you do, you would want me to be happy in this marriage as well. I keep stressing to you how miserable I am. I have had threesomes with you…for you. I have complimented other women."

"Yes, I'm fucking barren!" She continued, "I can't give you the family you want. Believe me that breaks my heart more than it does yours. But I have given you many supportive, loving years as your wife. And I just can't do this anymore. The same way I support you doing your first love which is film, you don't support me with mine which is music. Music was here before you. I was singing before I met you, that's how you know me...as a singer. That's who you know me to be!"

"So why would you want me to forget who I was and sweep it under the rug like I'm just a nobody," she continued. "It's like you want to shine...alone...and you want to shine brighter than me. You feel like my shining is on your arm, but I want to build *together*. If your idea of this is you shining and me tucked away following in your shadow, you can kick rocks."

This time when Ty left, he left for good. The divorce has been nasty and could possibly take years to settle. Kennedi isn't asking for much, but Ty doesn't want her to have anything.

Kennedi lost her husband because he was not understanding of her needs. She did the ultimate to please her man and it was never good enough. She was not willing to let him constantly berate her and keep her from doing what she felt she was born to do. She did not feel wanted, needed or desired.

Her husband wanted all of what he desired without compromise. Any type of relationship yields a certain amount of compromise. With marriage, especially, bringing together two lives to grow and move forward as one is a complicated thing to do. Both parties' feelings, goals and desires should be taken into account. Then the compromise can satisfy both the husband and wife to a point where there is happiness on both sides.

Since Ty wanted to have his cake and eat it too, Kennedi was left with no cake, just an empty plate watching Ty enjoy his. He heard her complaining, but didn't really listen to what she had to say. He was more busy thinking of a rebuttal, he was only hearing her to respond, not with the intent on making a change to see his wife happy.

So as you can see, it was easy for Daphne's words about following dreams to resonate with Kennedi at the bonfire. She's trying to figure out how to move forward, without Ty, while wondering if it will all be worth it in the end.

## PARIS

*The* next morning after the bonfire with Daphne and her crew, I woke up refreshed. It was a really good night of clean, honest fun. And so effortless. Dancing around barefoot in the sand without a care in the world seemed so easy with them. No pretenses, we could be ourselves, which is just what we did.

I left my room and walked into the kitchen. There were bowls of fresh fruit, cold mimosas and a sweet, balmy breeze that invited me out to the pool. I fixed a plate and peeked over the chef's shoulder to see what she was cooking up. Kennedi and Madison were already chillaxin' on cushy white pool chairs enjoying the scenery. Madison was used to being up early since she worked out at 5:30 most mornings in order to make it to the office before the good ol' white boys did.

"Morning, Divas." I lifted my mimosa to them.

"Hey girl," Kennedi crooned. It always sounded like she was singing. Even her speaking voice was amazing.

"Good morning, Lola!" Madison added.

"Last night was incredible," Kennedi started. "Low-key, English people know how to party."

"You mean people from across the pond, eh?" Madison said with a horrible English accent. We all laughed.

"So what's the game plan today, chicas?" British blasted. "I know you hoes planned something."

"The only hoe I see is you!" Kennedi said.

"Ya mama!" British retorted.

"You wouldn't be talking like that if Delores Gayle was in ya face," Kennedi said without skipping a beat.

"We have to be at the dock in two hours. The yacht is taking us sight-seeing. We'll get to do some swimming and a little shopping." I informed them of the plans.

"I know y'all can't wait to see me in my thong-th-thong, thong, thong," British sang. She stood up and started shaking her ass to a beat only she could hear in that crazy brain of hers. "British is a baaaad bitch!"

"British ain't nobody checkin' for no thots over here!" Kennedi said, standing up. "Me tink dey wan wine on de gyal," she pursed out duck lips, closed her eyes and rubbed her hands up and down her hips as she winded slowly. Me and Madison busted out laughing.

"Let me run to get some bills. Can I yank the string to pull the suit off?" a deep, male voice said. We all turned around and yelled, "OHHH!" It was Adler and Paris.

"Speaking of thots," British mumbled.

"Hey girls," Paris blushed. She pushed Adler toward the stairs that would lead him to the beach exit. He acted like he didn't want to leave. He could walk to his villa on the sand. We just looked at each other in silence, trying to hold in our laughter like little school girls until she waltzed back up the stairs. She looked at us all and dropped it like it was hot a few times.

"Actually, they like it like this!"

"AHHHHH!!" We all started screaming and clapping.

"You and Mr. Adler were dancing pretty hot and heavy last night, girl!" Madison started.

"We need deets!" I said sitting up in my chair, getting comfortable. I wanted all the tea. Hell, I was used to getting it anyway.

"There ain't no virgins in this crew. You all know what to do. All of ya!" Paris teased.

"I ain't never been with a white boy before," British said frowning up my face.

"Me either…until last night."

"Well, give us the damn tea girl! You trippin'!" British said. Paris told us all about her little escapade with the white boy. As she ran down the deets, the chef handed us plates that she fixed for us since we were too busy being nosey to notice breakfast was ready. She cooked us the fluffiest eggs known to man. They looked like yellow clouds on our plates. Everything was cooked to perfection.

We ran to our rooms, got changed and got our bags together, we were going to be gone all day. A taxi truck took us to the docks, then we boarded the yacht. In less than five minutes, we were cruising on the open water. The sound of the water lapping against the side of the vessel was drowned out by the radio jamming old school 90's melodies.

The captain took us to this gorgeous island with a huge bay speckled with smaller yachts, little boats and groups of people swimming and snorkeling. He walked us out to the front of the boat so we could see the throngs of people enjoying nature's beauty. Looking down, you could see schools of vibrantly colored fish moving around. The water was blue, but crystal clear.

"I wanna dive in!" Kennedi said.

"Not with this hair," Madison answered.

"Why would you come all the way to paradise and be too afraid to get your hair wet?" Kennedi asked.

"Girl, you know how we do!"

"Y'all wasting time talking...jeronimooooooo!"
Paris jumped in and allowed herself to plummet.

"How deep is it?" Kennedi turned to the
captain.

"Oh, not deep. Only about 35...45 feet."

"We all don't have that natural juices and
berries shit like Paris," British said. We watched Paris
sink deeper and deeper in the water. Her beautiful,
thick black hair compliments of her black father and
Puerto Rican mother floated in the water. She knew
how to swim, we weren't worried about that. There
was something about seeing her descend that made me
see the parallel with her life. Lemme give you the run
down on Paris.

Paris is messy. You know, the friend who is
always up in somebody else's business? Yeah, that's
her. She is a hair dresser by trade. Beauticians make
out these days. Looking at the cost of sew-ins and hair,
pockets get fat real quick.

Girls get their hair done every week. She has
heads lined up to be fried, dyed and laid to the side.
Paris is right there to get them straight. She is good at
what she does and is booked for months out. She only
works four days a week because she makes enough in
those four days. That's now. When she first got
started, she worked seven days a week, and what
seemed like 24 hours a day. The girl was on a mission.

Coming from Compton, she saw the worst of the worst. Paris knew what it was like to flip the switch on the wall and have no lights come on. She lived sometimes not knowing where her next meal was going to come from. It was just her and her father. Her mother, who gave her the Puerto Rican blood and a fiery attitude, passed away when Paris was a teen. Her father struggled to raise her. Battling the heartache of losing his wife, he also lost his job and had to rely on odd and end jobs to pay the bills.

My girl knew she was not about that life. She started doing hair in the hood and saved up money to get a cosmetology license. It worked. It got her out of the hood. Once she landed in a decent shop, she busted her ass to make money.

Compton never represented anything but pain for her after her mother died. The area was bad before then, but she didn't know anything different. Having her rock taken away from her, Paris couldn't wait to get the hell outta dodge. She set her sights on Atlanta and never looked back.

Paris was 19 in a strange city where she didn't know anybody. It felt good to have a new start. British met Paris when she sat in her chair. Both having an entrepreneurial spirit at such a young age, they were a rare breed. Naturally, British introduced me to Paris and the rest is history. The three of us became thick as thieves.

She never turned away a client. That's where all her messiness came from. Being around women all day, they had nothing to do but talk. Barber shops are the same way. Being in there, you get all the juicy gossip and what's going on in the streets.

Paris liked to have a good time. She worked hard for her money and believed that she earned the opportunity to spend it. Walking through Louis Vuitton, she looked for a new bag to add to her collection. She spotted the bag and a guy spotted her. She looked at him and through him. He was easily forgettable.

"That looks nice on you," he said as she tried it on to get a better gauge of how it felt.

"It better...for six G's."

"That's nothing to a boss like you," he laughed. "But I'd like to see you with it."

"Make it happen then," she looked him in his eyes. He took too long.

"Yeah, that's what I thought." Paris pulled the bag away from her and held it up to look at it again. "I'll take your word for it." Pairs handed the sales associate the bag, paid for it and was on her way out of the store. He followed her out of the store.

"So, when do I get to see you with it?"

"Here it is, I bought it." She held up the bag, then turned around and kept walking. Like I said, he was easily forgettable.

"I want to see *you* again." She looked a little confused, but gave him the digits. He called and took her out. It was a whirlwind romance. By that I mean, they moved very quickly, not that it was the sweep-a-girl-off-her-feet type of love.

Trey was a sports agent. True to form, he fit the bill. He played basketball in college, but things just didn't work out for him at the next level. Rather than sulk in not going pro, he found a few players who needed representation. He had a winning smile, was very neat, his clothes were always immaculate and he was well groomed. He wasn't easy on the eyes, but he could dress! Trey was well put together.

He wasn't the super romantic type, but neither was Paris. The whole PDA, lovey dovey thing just wasn't them. They quickly settled into a comfortable relationship. He kept his home and space, so did she. He traveled working deals for his athletes; Paris worked her butt off gaining and maintaining clients. It was the perfect set up. They found that one person who they knew they could count on in each other, who could listen to them air their frustrations, and make love without being smothered in a relationship.

The talks about marriage were cool. Paris was good thinking her man was making honest money. He didn't make as much as his athletes, but his money was good and it was long. He was not frugal, but he didn't blow money on stupid shit either. She wouldn't have to work so hard.

They finally moved together to a big house. Trey insisted that they get a house to grow into. Paris could have done without the library and two offices that she knew would remain unused and dusty. She knew that her snatch was not going to birth enough kids to fill up five bedrooms either.

Since it was just two of them, chances were when they were home together, they would want to be in the same room. Trey wanted to impress his current and potential clients. He wanted them to see just how well he was doing which would make them feel more confident in his ability to represent them. Trey would have it no other way. Since he was handling the bills, Paris shut up about it.

They were so funny. The wedding was a tiny intimate ceremony with just Paris, Trey, and their parents. They wore the tiniest of wedding bands. These days, chicks get married and want the biggest rock to flaunt the fact that they have been taken off the market. Not Paris. That's probably one of the things he appreciated about her. She seemed to be low maintenance. Her announcement to the shop was real matter-of-fact.

"Hey Paris!" The greeting was scattered around the salon on a Tuesday when she walked in.

"I's married nah!" She held up her left hand. You could feel the wind as everybody snapped their necks to look at her.

"Whaaaaaaat?"

"No you didn't!"

"When the hell did that happen?"

"I know you didn't get married without me!"

"How about a congratulations, ladies?" Paris answered.

"Oh, yeah," they clamored over to her to hug and kiss her, expressing their congratulations.

"Why did y'all just run away like that? What is there to hide?" A faithful customer asked.

"We didn't run away. We just wanted to have something small and private."

"That's just a mess there!" the customer said.

"So, tell us about it, girl," a beautician piped up.

"Well," Paris smiled and signaled a client to hop in her chair, "we went to the courthouse yesterday. Our parents were there, that's all we wanted."

"All *he* wanted..."

"No, both of us," Paris insisted.

"Paris, no little girl dreams of getting married in a damn courthouse." The wash girl interjected. She stood in the middle of the salon with her arms stretched wide. "We grow up wanting to wear a beautiful, white, sexy princess gown with a veil saying 'I Do' in front of a room full of our friends and family. Then, feeding each other cake and shaking what our mamas gave us until it's time to pop that thang for our new husband!" She bent over and shook her ass. She got hi-fives from the other stylists.

"While people talk shit about your dress...and what they would have done differently...and what your cake looked like...and how much money you spent?" Paris added, "Chile please! I'm not paying for y'all cheap heffas to talk shit about me and not even bring a gift!"

"You don't call us cheap when we pay to sit our asses in your chair." They all laughed.

He seemed sweet enough. From time to time, Trey would go into the salon just to say 'hi' or bring her lunch. He definitely caught the attention of the ladies when he did that. They dove into a talking frenzy when he left. He'd stroll on in, looking fly as ever, you know, business casual like.

"Here are some beautiful white gardenias to brighten up your day, Babe!" He would tease, hug her from behind and kiss her neck. "See you when you get home," and just as quickly as he walked in, he was on his way out.

"Oooooh, girl!" The wash girl started, "I can't even get my baby daddy to call just to say hi without asking for some ass."

"I know that's right," a customer agreed.

"You got that nigga sprung girl!"

"Paris gon' be running home to drop them draws!"

"He dresses nice too."

"Thanks, Boo!" Paris was smiling from ear to ear.

"Maybe a little too nice," a stylist said.

"What?" Paris put her flat iron down and looked at the stylist who made the last comment.

"I just said, he dresses *too* nice."

"Why? 'Cause you can't see nuts hanging all out of skinny jeans that sag down to his ankles and wife beaters, he dresses too nice?"

"No, but he is wearing skinny slacks...I'm just saying," the stylist hit Paris with the Kanye shrug.

"Shut up! You just hatin' 'cause ain't no man coming up in here checking for you, Boo Boo, ok?" Another stylist chimed in backing Paris up.

"Yeah," Paris said. "Let's talk about the real issue. Your ass ain't got no man in sight! Yet, you feel the need to pick apart my man. Do you want me to find you one like mine?"

"Paris, go on before I hurt your feelings," the stylist sad.

"Whatever chick!" Paris said rolling her eyes.

"Right, whatever."

Shortly after celebrating their one year anniversary, Paris became pregnant. She was excited, although just like anyone who is without kids, she was accustomed to being free. Having a child would pin her down to a schedule and she would have to cut down on the amount of clients she took. Trey was thrilled! He hoped that they had a daughter so he could dress her up and take her around with him.

Being that he had a number of his clients with him at any given time, Paris told him she didn't think it was a good idea to keep their child in the streets with him, boy or girl. The sex was yet to be determined, but Trey stepped up even more. He'd call to check on her, see if she needed anything while at the shop. Whatever she said the baby wanted, he brought her at the drop of a hat. He calmed down his travel schedule and arranged for meetings to be done over the phone when possible so he could be there just in case something happened.

By the second trimester, Paris had cravings for green beans and lemon juice. Even the other moms thought that was a weird combination, but eating just about anything else made her throw up. With the exception of fresh fruit.

She had such a strong desire for lemon juice that she carried the small plastic lemons in her purse and squeezed so much in her bottles of water that the water was cloudy like lemonade. If Trey couldn't get to her, he sent one of his athletes, friends, or even one of the guys who were hoping to get on his client roster.

Paris felt kind of strange having random young men coming to her job bringing her food and different treats. The guys, mostly being athletes and trainers, looked like beef-cakes with tight bodies sauntering their fine asses into the salon. Of course they commanded attention. The ladies went crazy, practically dropping their panties on the floor. Poor guys didn't even realize they were about to slip in drool.

When they found out the sex of the baby was a girl, Trey got uber excited. He took over decorating the nursery. He told Paris not to worry about a thing! And she didn't. Trey planned a shower and invited all the stylists from the salon, along with some of the clients. He even invited a few of his own clients and their significant others. He left no detail undone. Everything from the invitations to the centerpieces to parting gifts were in line with the signature Tiffany & Co. teal baby shower. Trey spared no expense embellishing the arrival of his future princess, much more than he did for his own wedding.

"Your husband did all of this?" Everybody was so surprised that a man would go to such a great length for a shower.

When Baby Amarii was born, nothing else mattered to Trey. Nothing. His whole world revolved around her. It was a surprise that he had made it past 30 without having any children, especially as a young, black man who was educated and had ends rolling in.

As new parents, everywhere they went, he wanted Amarii with them. At first it was cute, then it became kind of frustrating. Not that Paris didn't want her daughter around, she missed being able to spend time with her husband. Paris felt like he could have easily let their nanny, Miranda watch Amarii so they could have some alone time. Trey felt that their baby should be with them as much as possible.

"How are you getting adjusted to mommy hood?" One of Paris's clients, Niecey asked.

"People said I wouldn't get any sleep, chile that was an understatement! I ain't had sleep since sleep had me." The ladies laughed.

"Be glad you don't have a colicky baby!" Another client yelled across the salon. "Those babies never shut up!"

"Amarii is a good baby. She's not fussy at all, but her daddy doesn't want to be without her."

"It's still new. Chile, trust me when I tell you it'll wear off."

"I don't know 'bout that one. He refuses to put her in a regular daycare. Trey only has a nanny in the house four days a week and half of the time, he lets her go home because one of us is home. Anywhere we go, Amarii has to come. I miss having alone time with my man."

"She's only a few months old, right?"

"Eight...eight months. I don't think we've been alone since she was born. Literally. Amarii is always there."

"Why don't you plan something with just the two of you and tell him you made arrangements for the nanny to stay with the baby."

"Thanks, I will. Now, let's get into Shemika's man slithering all up in Giselle's DM's."

"Ooooh no ma'am!" the client said. She knew Paris was about to dish.

"Yes, girl! On Instagram. Giselle showed me Shemika's man, Reshaud, trying to put in some work.

"O...M...G! What did the messages say?"

Paris held no punches. She told Niecey pretty much verbatim what the messages said. See what I'm talking about? Messy! She was talking low so others couldn't hear her, but you can bet those other women turned on their supersonic hearing, Mr. Potato Head ears.

Paris was glad she vented to Niecey about her own situation. She listened to the advice. The next week, Paris made a reservation at one of Trey's favorite restaurants. Every 10 minutes, he called or texted the nanny. He kept shifting his weight around in the chair as if he was uncomfortable, looking around nervously. It made Paris feel very awkward.

"Wassup with you?" she finally asked. She had done her best to overlook it, but she was bothered.

"What do you mean, Sweetie?"

"You acting all funny like the only thing that matters is Amarii. Ummm, hello? Your wife is right here!"

"I know, I know. But, I feel like no one can take care of your baby the way you do. I just want to make sure she's ok."

"You found Miranda. You hired her. Didn't you have her checked out?"

"Yeah, yeah, got her to sign a confidentiality agreement...the whole nine."

"Ok, Trey. Let's focus on us. Just because we have a baby now doesn't mean we have to lose who we are as a couple."

The next week, Paris got dolled up. She let the owner of the shop hook her hair up and slipped into a cute dress that was blousy on the top and tight to show her hips and legs. Paris had always been curvy and she embraced those curves. She called into Trey's closet where he was getting ready.

"Sweetie! Hurry up, Miranda will be here soon so we can go."

"Oh yeah," he started, "I told her to come with us," Paris looked up in the direction of the stairs where his voice was trailing.

"Huh?"

"Yeah, I meant to tell you."

"Why? I told you before that I had already spoken to her."

"I think it's cool if she comes to dinner with us. That way Amarii can be attended to, but we still get some time out of the house."

"Hell no! Tonight was supposed to be our night! It's not about Amarii being attended to, but giving us time to reconnect," Paris urged. *Ding dong!*

Miranda was already at the door, she walked right in. Miranda was younger than Trey and Paris. She was happy to get the job and came highly recommended. The family she worked for before them moved out of the country. Visiting Europe was one thing, moving was another.

Miranda had a warm spirit and gave Amarii her full attention. She was also crunk that this job could potentially have her around ball players. She was banking on that, literally. She respected their marriage, wasn't gunning for Trey, but his athletes were up for grabs. She was just a young girl trying to get on.

"Paris, how are you?"

"Good, Miranda. How are you?" Paris responded blandly to her blonde nanny, with an instant 'tude.

"Ooh, I can't wait to see where Trey takes us tonight."

"*We* are going to Julio's, I made arrangements for two. But, thank you for agreeing to stay here with Amarii."

"Trey invited me to come with you all. Honey child, I want me some hibachi." Paris stared at her obvious attempt to 'sound black'.

"I made reservations for the two of us at Julio's. That's where we're going, I'll get you a gift card for hibachi."

"Julio's can wait!" Trey said, neither of the ladies heard him come down the stairs. Paris was pissed all over again.

"You taking her side over mine?"

"Paris, don't be ridiculous. I want hibachi too, actually." She didn't even want to go anymore. Paris had to tell the girls at the shop to find out if her man was the only one who carried on like that.

The shop is where she came alive. She had to be there. Being around those girls had become her life. Trey and Paris were becoming more and more like roommates. Working around all those women gave her insight on her marriage. Wrong or right, she got to see how others thought.

"Alright y'all, check this one out. So last night, my girl made plans for her and her hubs to go to dinner. He paid for a babysitter to go with them so their daughter could still be with them on the date!" She spoke with an attitude of disbelief.

"Oh hell naw!" There was a collective groaning around the room.

"I know right?" Paris egged on. She needed to know what to think.

"No ma'am!" one of the stylists echoed.

"Why would he even want a babysitter there?" A client asked.

"Wait," another stylist paused the convo. "So, let me get this straight. It was her...her husband...a babysitter and the daughter?"

"Yes!"

"Awwww!" The response was collective disappointment, yet again.

"Sounds to me like her husband don't wanna be 'round her," the client said.

"Most men try to run away from their kids, not want to keep them around!" another client added.

"That's bullshit. Something in the milk ain't clean!" roared one of the stylists.

"Like what though? I thought it was messed up, but I didn't know what to tell her."

"He's obviously trying to put some space between him and his wife. For what reason, we don't know enough to know," the stylist said.

"Hmmm." Paris sat in her chair and spun facing the mirror. She was mad at herself for not stepping up and handling the situation then, she should have put her foot down. She would rather just roll with the punches than have him upset at her; but, something had to be said.

The conversations swirled around her. She was so naïve to what was going on in her marriage. She just couldn't put her finger on the problem. She did know that she was not happy. He had to be screwing another woman, she just had to find out who it was. Then do what? What was she going to do? She wasn't going to leave. They had a young child and she was still in love. Paris needed to make herself more irresistible.

When she got home that night, Paris mentioned the whole date fiasco to Trey. He brushed her off and told her she was making a big deal out of nothing. He told her to just chill out because they spent time together at home so missing one date night was not going to hurt them. He assured her the next one she planned would be just the two of them.

It wasn't. The nanny seemed to be coming around more and more. She asked him if he was afraid to be alone with her, since there seemed to always be another body around. When Paris raised hell about it, Trey started spending more time away from the house. Working. It's like she couldn't win for losing. She wanted to continue to strengthen the bond with the husband who insisted on not being alone with her. When she complained about it, he spent more time away. Paris was losing the friend she thought she had.

Trey's job as a sports agent could have been done anywhere. He had done well for himself and set up a nice, cozy office in the house. Everything he needed was there. Computers, fax machine, printers, cameras to have meetings where he could actually see the people he spoke to.

The people, however, were not there. He had to be in the field to gain the trust of recruits to take them from being potential clients to signing with him. Meeting with coaches, team owners, and managers always worked better over golf or scotch. He directed more of his attention to traveling.

Miranda was down for the cause. He planned his trips to be day trips or maybe stay over one night. He didn't take Amarii to the course with him, but she was in a room nearby. Paris wasn't exactly thrilled with him taking the baby on business trips. However, she was in good company with the nanny, so it wasn't too bad. It gave Paris a much needed breather.

He clearly wasn't interested in working on their marriage. Not work in the sense that they were having problems, but work in the way of investing time and effort in maintaining their connection. They didn't talk much anymore, surely weren't kicking it anymore and the sex…forget about it!

Paris couldn't understand why he seemed to be so turned off. Their sex life had been on point. Then things started to become sporadic. So sporadic that Paris started keeping a log of every time they had sex. It was ridiculous. Once a month! If that! What man only wanted sex from his wife once a month? It was bad enough having to deal with the physical changes that accompanied becoming a mother, he sure wasn't doing anything to reassure her that she was still attractive in his eyes.

She figured she'd work on her body. Paris joined a local boot camp workout. Exercise was going to be her new best friend. It was tough finding the time, but she rushed out of work yelling, "Gotta go get my sexy on girls!" She was dedicated to working out twice a week and drinking fresh fruit smoothies in the morning for breakfast. The first 20 pounds shed off easily, then it tapered off. Still with a goal of 15 pounds left to lose, she was already feeling herself. Her attitude showed it.

Now, with Trey spending more time away from the house, she had to make the best of times when he was there. She would climb into bed and spoon behind him, rubbing her hands up and down his tall, slender physique. Then she'd find her way down to his manhood, groping him to get him in the mood. He usually laid there until he was fully erect, then turn over and let her climb on top of him.

Paris sensually rode him back and forth until she came, then he nudged her off of him, next he'd bend her over and sexed her hard from behind until he came. While he pounded her, she felt totally distant, empty. There was no passion, no sensuality, just fucking. It was like, he was doing her a favor by having sex to begin with.

Their sex life had become so dry and emotionless. Paris really wanted it, she craved physical attention from Trey. She wanted to be held, to be caressed. He just seemed to do what he had to do to keep from catching blue balls. Questions begun to plague her mind about where he was getting loving from. They were barely 35, he was still a young, virile man with needs. He had to be cheating, that was the only logical answer.

"Aight chicas! Let's talk about this situation I heard on the radio today," Paris started while working on a sew-in. There was definitely time to kill. "This girl called in and said she and her husband just had a baby, like a year or two ago I can't remember. Anyway, her husband doesn't want sex anymore."

"Ooooh, he cheatin' girl! He cheatin'!" Insisted a client who was getting finger waves with a streak of red.

"That's the only answer. He's getting it from somewhere else."

"What man turns down the pooh-na-nny? Nuh uh," said the wash girl.

"These men don't appreciate what our bodies go through to have their babies! The stretch marks, the gas, the cravings, the emotional mood swings, the swelling..."

"Chile, I was so jacked up when I was pregnant, I would see a lotion commercial and bust out crying. I was hot all the time, just walking around ripping damn clothes off!" Laughed a client.

"They don't give a damn! I've been thinking about getting a boob job," one of the stylists said.

"Huh?" Paris asked in disbelief.

"Yeah, girl! I breastfed three churrin', and honey these mom boobs don't see nothing but the flo'!" They all hollered. The conversation kept going about post-baby bodies, but Paris was stuck on the cheating part.

When she thought about it, it seemed plausible, but it didn't seem likely. Unless Miranda was doing more than changing Amarii's diapers when she was traveling with Trey. He didn't seem any different. None of his patterns changed, really. Except the sex. Maybe she needed to get one of those mommy makeover surgeries to do some nipping, tucking and lifting.

"...Crumwell. He is a girl, I'm telling ya!" A client was holding her phone, laughing loudly. All Paris heard was Crumwell and it snapped her out of her daze.

"What? What did you say about Crumwell?"

"I'm looking at CelebMail. They put up a post about Thaddeus Crumwell with his agent and a few other guys and I said they are all queens."

"No they aren't!" Paris sat up in her chair instantly defensive.

"Yes hunnn! My cousin is gay. He knows Thad personally. Thad likes the D."

"My husband is his agent."

"Is this your husband?" The client handed Paris the phone.

"Yes."

"Well...I don't know what to tell ya."

"How y'all gon' sit here and...y'all know my husband ain't gay! You just sitting there, letting this bitch talk about my..."

"Bitch? I didn't do shit to you! Don't be mad at me because ya man likes men!"

Paris jumped out of her seat. She was done. She couldn't believe what was happening. The chick was talking sideways out of her mouth about Trey and nobody was stopping her. Nobody was defending him.

Paris got her shit and left. She didn't want to be around those messy bitches. They lived for some tea whether it was true of not. Paris knew they were just jealous because on the outside it looked like she had the perfect life, complete with a husband who was hard working and took care of her. He loved their daughter, had good credit, bought her a beautiful house and waited on her damn near hand and foot.

She thought the surgery thing out and figured it would give her some well-deserved time away from those catty bitches to put some space between them.

One day, Paris looked in the mirror. She slowly took her clothes off to get into the shower. The water ran hot and steam bellowed out of the glass and marble shower. Standing in front of the bay window mirror, she looked at her body. Her face looked young, she was aging very well. She knew she was pretty, men and women told her so every day. She slid her pants off and turned around. Her legs looked good. A few dimples on her ass, but not bad, most women had them. She slipped off her shirt, pulled down the straps on her bra and unhooked it.

Staring at her boobs in the mirror, they had a natural sag. She didn't breastfeed long, they weren't destroyed, but they didn't sit up like they used to. She was 35 after all. She put two fingers under one breast and lifted it up slightly, then smiled.

Her gaze drifted down to the stretch marks on her stomach. There was nothing so bad that could make her understand why Trey acted like he didn't want to touch her. She turned around again, arched her back and put those same two fingers under her butt to lift it up higher. A faint smile crossed her lips.

Paris got in the shower and let drops from the shower head wash her cares down the drain. She inhaled the steam deeply and exhaled slowly. She needed love. She needed attention. She had no clue of how to regain her husband's interest. She took down the removable shower head and let it make love to her. She put it on her vagina and changed the water to a pulsating spray. After she came, she took her shower.

She decided to go ahead with the surgery. She went in for a consultation and turned out to be a great candidate for the procedure. Going under for an elective procedure is a big deal and Paris was well aware that anything could go wrong. They made her sign her life away saying as such. It seemed so easy to do. So many women were doing it. With a new ass and high, bouncy boobs, she was sure Trey would find whatever he was looking for in her.

Everything went off without a hitch. Paris had the work done and was very happy with the results. Trey helped by staying with her to help her recoup after surgery. He wasn't being a total asshole. Miranda helped, too. The two of them made sure she had everything she needed while she was down. Amarrii was too young to understand that her mom could not pick her up, so Miranda would sit her on the couch next to Paris to feel her warmth.

Over the course of the next three weeks, the ladies bonded. It was still very much a professional relationship, but with nothing but time and space between them, they did a lot of getting to know each other. Paris was grateful that Trey suggested Miranda and Amarii stay there with her.

Paris noticed that Trey barely said a word about her new boobs and augmented ass. Everybody else sure did. It made her feel good that her body looked better. They both were a natural fit for her, just enhanced what she already had. Trey did not pay her any more attention. They were still only having sex, painstakingly, once a month. Yet, it seemed like sex seemed to be the only topic of conversation around her.

"I'm sorry I'm late!" A client rushed into the shop. "I overslept!"

"It's 10:00, that's not an early. You shoulda took your lil' self to sleep last night. Mmmm hmm," the receptionist replied.

"My man wants to screw me all the time! He kept me up all damn night." She sounded exasperated.

"He should, right?" her stylist said.

"I guess, but damn! A sista needs a break!"

"If he gets a break from you, what do you think he's going to do?"

"What do you mean?" The client looked in the mirror at her stylist who worked in the station next to Paris.

"Play dumb if you want to," the stylist adjusted her client's head back where she wanted it. "If he ain't getting it from you, he'll get it somewhere else."

"Sometimes, they just don't want it," Paris said.

"What man over the age of 13 don't want a piece of ass? They'll take it in their sleep, they'll take it before they eat, after they eat, in the car, on the dresser, before work…"

"On my fiancée's days off, if I have to work, I go home on my lunch break with two extra value meals, 2 cokes and a smile. I tell him, he better get this snatch before my fries get cold!" They all busted out laughing, except Paris.

"Things change so much after a baby," Paris volunteered.

"True, it takes some time getting back to normal, but honey listen. Ray Ray is such a freak, that fool couldn't even wait the whole six weeks. That nigga told me straight up he was going to find him some booty if I didn't give it up." The client sat there a moment in thought, "Lil' Mama came ten months after Xander." All the ladies laughed again.

"Damn! It took me and my hubs about a year to get back to normal," a client volunteered. Paris didn't say anything, just kept doing hair. She had become much more reserved, especially since the client pulled up the CelebMail post in front of the girls. The surgery was a cry for help. She was quickly losing herself all the while trying *not* to lose her husband. In the meantime, he was gearing up for a weeklong trip out to Paris.

"Paris? You have to go all the way to Paris?" *Are NBA teams offering green cards*, she thought. Six months before, she would have spoken her mind. Now, she didn't have the heart. It was like walking on eggshells dealing with him.

"Some of the team owners and managers are having a serious private meeting about the future of the league."

"I don't have to go to the meetings, I can get some shopping in. We can do some couple shit. How can you go to the city of my name sake and not take me with you?"

"Paris," he looked at her in the eyes, almost as if he was disappointing himself by having to tell her, "look. It's going to be all guys. The meeting is private, which is why they're having it out of the country. If all of the guys show up in the city with their women, how do you think that's going to look? Can't bring attention to ourselves flying in like that."

"Sounds like you really just don't want me there."

"Paris. Thad is coming. I told you he was thinking about transitioning to the business side. I'll keep in touch like I always do, but this meeting is strictly business."

He checked in to let her know he had landed and FaceTimed Amarii. She cooed and smiled seeing Daddy. Paris had some big news of her own. She was booked on a photoshoot for a music video. Those types of jobs pay well and the connections are priceless.

Paris walked onto the set and was ushered over to wardrobe, hair and makeup. No sooner than she walked in, she saw Hendrixx. Yes, he spelled his name with two x's on the end.

Hendrixx didn't ooze uber gay in his appearance, but honey when he spoke the first word, the jig was up! He looked like he got a fresh cut every three days. Never needed a cut, line, or an edge. Nothing. His clothes were always pristine. Hendrixx was certainly one of the most talented stylists around. Clients booked him, flying him all over the country to style them. He was paid too.

"Hey bitch-uh!" He screamed when he saw Paris. There was no bass in his voice. They were laughing, *kee kee* cool, not BFF cool. They had worked a few clients together in the past.

"Hendriiiiiiiiiiixx!" she laughed.

"Yes-uh! Honey, chum on' show a bitch some love!" They did the air cheek kiss thing. Paris got herself settled in, got her assignments and waited on the first video model to plop in the chair.

"So what has been going on doll?"

"Not much love, trying to make this money. What about you?"

"The same," he giggled. "Trying to get these coinzzzzz-uh. I needs my checks rolling in." He pushed back his clear framed glasses. No prescription, they just popped with his outfit.

"Shit, I feel ya."

"How is that baby of yours? I see you got some new babies. Them ta-tas is sitting right gurrrrl." Hendrixx gave a little shimmy.

"Oh chile, Amarii is fine. She's one now, well, 16 months." They continued on having surface small talk throughout the day. It was always fun being around Hendrixx. He was a live wire. He also spilled tea...all of it...on everybody. He was such a queen, and everybody knew he ran his mouth, but he kept on getting all the good deets. He didn't care whose name he dropped.

"They need to come on, girl, I got to go. Low key, I'm hopping on a red eye to Paris."

"Paris?" She thought it was odd that two men in her life were going to Paris at the same time.

"No tea, but I'm hopping on a flight to Paris with my boo."

"The same one from the Pretty Sista Magazine shoot last year?"

"Ooh no! He was trash like holey draws!" He pursed his lips and tilted his head. "This one is Thaddeus and he is fo-ine….fine! Chile, he runs up and down the court like nobody's business."

"He's in the league?"

"Crumwell." *BOOM!* Thaddeus Crumwell, America's heartthrob was Trey's biggest client.

"Oh really? Yes, him and a few other girls are flying over. We're doing a weeklong getaway!"

"Paris will be nice," she managed. Paris was weak. She didn't know how to ask who else was going, because by 'girls' she knew what he really meant. Was Trey going to be there? Were the ladies in the shop right? It was all too much to deal with, but she had to squeeze out as much as she could.

"It will be, but we have to do it over there so we can do it big. Over here, these folks be all in ya business."

"My husband, is flying over for…"

"Trey? Mmm hmm, I know." *BOOM!* Paris could barely breathe. It couldn't be true. It wasn't true. But, Hendrixx was talking to her like it was nothing, like he expected her to know. There was no way her husband was gay. They used to have sex all the time. They even had a baby. It wasn't possible. It just wasn't. She didn't know how to go about finding the truth. If she asked, of course he would say no. But why would he marry her if he wasn't in love with her? If he wasn't attracted to her? It just didn't make any sense.

She tried to play it smart. This was not a conversation to have over the phone, or FaceTime. His being away would give her time to work things out in her head. What to say. What to do. How to react. When they did speak, she asked baiting questions to pull deets out of him. When they FaceTimed, she observed his surroundings hoping to see a glimpse of something out of place or any tell-tale signs. Nothing.

The week crept by and when he made it home, Miranda and Amarii were there to greet him. Paris had to work. He spent two days being jet lagged, so they saw each other and held light convos, then he was back to sleep and she was off to work. On the third day, when Paris came home, she decided she was going to confront him. She had to ask. Had to. She had finally gotten up the nerve. Except Miranda was there with Amarii.

"Paris, we need to talk." Miranda barked as soon as Paris walked in the door. That was not her usual greeting or demeanor. Miranda was always pleasant and always upbeat.

"Where is Amarii?" Paris immediately noticed how quiet it was.

"She's in her crib taking a late nap."

"Ok…" Paris spoke very cautiously.

"When Trey came home the other day…he, they…Thad…"

"Spit it out."

"I saw him and Thad…you know, together."

"No, I don't know."

"They were together, making out."

"Making out?" It took a second for her to process what she was hearing.

"Thad was in the car that dropped Trey off that morning. What was that?" Miranda looked up in the air like she was thinking, "Tuesday? Yeah, Tuesday. At first, I caught them just like pecking. They saw me and stopped, then Trey pulled Thaddeus and they just started going at it. Like grabbing dicks and…"

"I get! I get it!" Paris couldn't catch the tears before they fell.

"I know I'm going to lose my job for telling you this, especially since I signed a non-disclosure, but sista to sista, I had to tell you what's going on."

"Sista to sis…" Her voice trailed off, "Miranda you're white."

"Well, woman to woman. I think that's disgusting for him to carry on like that and you not know. It's been hell for me to keep this from you. But he's always been in the house every day when you came home from work. Anyway, I don't think they went on a business trip, there was another flamboyantly gay guy with him."

Paris staggered back. She couldn't even keep her footing. Miranda grabbed her arm and put her in a chair. Paris completely crumbled in her nanny's arms. Paris stopped breathing and started crying all at the same time. She didn't know what to do or how to feel. She was completely caught off guard. She glanced up at Miranda through a wall of tears in her eyes. She just started shaking her head.

She was so embarrassed. Clearly, she was the last to know. How could this be happening to her? What had she done wrong? Were there any signs she missed? Did she really just find out from the nanny? Her mind was swirling in a thousand different directions. She went from hurt to pain to disappointment to fear. Paris was completely overwhelmed. Miranda rubbed her back. Of course, she wanted to give her boss words of encouragement. In that moment, there was nothing to say.

"I'll take Amarii home with me tonight," Miranda said not seeking approval. Paris was too weak to even object. "...and I'm returning this Chanel to Trey. I can't be bought." Miranda placed a bag on the coffee table. Paris just cried harder.

Paris made her way into her bedroom. It was adjacent to the living room where they were. She threw herself on the bed. She cried and cried. It was like the sorrow of her soul was pouring out.

She reflected on so many conversations, mannerisms, him not wanting to be with her and it all made sense. Thinking back on all of the jokes, snide remarks and snickers at the salon, she could see now what everybody else seemed to have already known. She had been so naïve. She let Trey dictate so much of the marriage, but she was his beard.

She knew she needed to pull herself together. There weren't many things that would help her calm down, but a bubble bath guaranteed to soothe her somewhat. She pulled candles from her nightstand, along with the lighter. It was the kind with the extended piece so she didn't have to hold it close. It was ideal for candle lighting, which she did on a regular basis.

Paris pressed the flicker. *My husband is gay.* Flick! *When was he sleeping with these men?* Flick! *He knew he was gay when he married me.* Flick! *Muthafucka!* Flick! *What am I going to tell our daughter?* Flick! *I don't want her around that shit.* Flick! *Down low brotha, huh?* Flick! *Where was he sleeping with them?* Flick! *I hope not in my house!* Flick! *Did he fuck men in my bed?* Flick! *In* our *bed?* Flick! *Why is this happening to me?* Flick! *I can't sleep on this bed, these sheet.* Flick! *He probably fucked them in my bed!* Flick!

"I can't sleep on this fucking bed anymore!" Paris screamed. Her words seemed to echo off the walls. *Flick!* "Fuck somebody else on this bed now, muthafucka!" Paris stood there watching her bed burn. She threw up right next to it, then crumpled down to the floor.

She clearly was too distressed to comprehend her actions. She laid there inconsolable...until she saw smoke. She smelled it, but it didn't register. Paris turned around and saw her bed bellowing with smoke. How flammable silk sheets and Egyptian cotton drapes were was the last thing on her heartbroken mind. It seemed unreal how quickly the fire spread.

Paris saw the fire crawling up the walls and panic suddenly set in. She stood up, then fell because her legs were weak. She slinked over to the chaise and used it to pull herself up to a standing position then ran out of the room. She grabbed the handrail and hurried up the stairs to get Amarii. She rushed to the crib and saw Amarii was gone and panicked even more. Her heart was beating out of her chest, she frantically looked for Amarii in the room thinking she had gotten out of the crib.

"Miranda," she said, breathing a huge sigh of relief. Paris got the hell outta there. Not before noticing how fast her entire bottom floor was becoming engulfed in flames. The smoke was so thick, she could barely see the door. She got out and realized the only thing she had were the clothes on her back. She raced back in to pick up her purse. Thankfully it wasn't far from the door.

Standing across the street, she heard the sound of her windows breaking out. The fire was now breathing. Neighbors checked on her, sat her down on the grass and called the fire department. She was in awe of what was happening. Paris couldn't even process it.

She called me and all she could say was, "Come." I kept asking questions and got no response. When I heard the sirens in the background, I hopped my ass in the car and made it to her house in 10 minutes flat. The drive is normally double that.

Paris sat there, on the grass at her neighbors' house until long after all the flames were out. I let The Divas know what was going on. It was painful. All I knew was my girl's house had burned down, didn't know anything about Trey at that time. The house was almost completely engulfed in flames.

When I arrived, it seemed the firefighters were only just starting to fight the blaze. I sat down next to my friend. She felt so fragile in my hands. Amarii's room was directly on top of her and Trey's room. Both were a total loss, so was the living room and kitchen. The other rooms, including Trey's office weren't destroyed by fire. What the fire didn't get, the water did.

The police and fire marshal asked questions, took a written statement and told her about the overall process. I insisted that she come to my house. My boys were old enough to not want to be bothered with us, so she was safe to mourn her house in peace.

I took off work the next day to be with her. She told me everything. Since I was there when she was questioned, I knew she lied to the police saying a candle turned over and started it. They didn't buy her story, launched an investigation and charged her with arson.

The Divas were devastated. It was horrible seeing our friend like that. The first call she was allowed to make was to her lawyer. I had already done that. Madison was on the case.

It was a tense few months. Trey found out what Paris knew, he filed for divorce and custody of the child, citing she was emotionally unstable and about to stand trial for arson. The courts gave temporary custody to him until the arson case was finished. Even though he made significantly more than his wife, he didn't want to pay any alimony or child support.

She did not pose a flight risk, so she was able to be free while the case was ongoing. Her father went to court with her every day, so did Sade. They were there to show support. Meanwhile, the blogs were blowing up, *Top Agent Trey Barnes's Wife Burns House Down After Catching Him In Bed With Gay Lover.*

Surprisingly, the stylists from the shop also showed up to give support. The first day, they all came, cancelled all of their clients to be there for their sista. Faithful clients came. Miranda came as well.

Paris was so overwhelmed by the love. She broke down crying when she walked into the courtroom and saw her support system. Pitbull Madison used Miranda as the key witness in the trial to attest to Paris' mental state at the time of the fire. Madison didn't say Paris did not intentionally set the blaze, but she created enough reasonable doubt making the candle story plausible.

Her not-guilty verdict was read just days before we started planning the trip. It was also the catalyst for the trip. The Divas had to do a mild intervention to get her back on track. Not only had Paris lost her husband, but she lost everything she had.

See, Paris lost her husband because he was gay. Period. What he wanted, she simply could not offer other than someone to cover up his lifestyle. He never asked her to cover for him, he just assumed he could work out whatever he needed to. He really needed her more than she needed him...she was just not aware of what was going on.

She had become a fractured shell of who she used to be. She had been drowning in keeping up a façade of a happy, healthy marriage, then floundering in a sea of pseudo-happiness on her way to divorce court with a poor self-image.

Paris needs to be honest with herself, find out who she is and what she wants. She didn't want to be divorced. She didn't sign up for marriage, just to end up on the wrong side of it with a gay husband. Paris still was not over Trey. I think anybody could understand why.

## LOLA

*The* next day, we did a little shopping. We each got trinkets to remember our girls' excursion in the islands. Decorative coconut shells with beautiful pictures carved into them and gorgeous pictures of now familiar landscape. Madison grabbed her step-daughters keychains with some sort of colored liquid to divide the "water" from the "sky" and tiny boats, so the boats appeared to be floating on water. She bought her step-son pens that lit up with each pen stroke; all bearing the island's name.

We stopped at a food stand on the side of the road. They served fruit, hot food, as well as beer. It looked like a happening little spot. There was music blasting and the locals were not shy. As they waited in line, they were singing and dancing to the music. The women cooking on the make shift stove were singing and dancing as well. They all had a carefree attitude.

I was the first one off the taxi. As soon as I got off, I hopped right into the rhythm with them. They could tell we were tourists and were instantly tickled. After four days, I felt like I had some of that Carribbean 'riddum' flowing through my own veins. Their beats were as fresh and lively as the bright colors they wore. The Divas jumped off and right into a step with me.

It was so amazing being right there on the side of the road giving a shimmy, in a warm sun and salty breeze. The locals gave new meaning to the phrase, 'Don't worry, be happy'.

We tried to tell Paris not to chug her beer so fast. We had already done our routine of taking shots on the boat while skirting on open water past other islands, so we were feeling pretty nice. Then here she comes downing a beer like water. She drank the first one so fast, a bead of water ran from the bottle, down her arm and she was finished before the droplet hit the ground. She barely even touched her food. After that Paris began dancing with a man whispering sweet island *tings* in her ear and she didn't know what he was saying. They were speaking more through the movement of their hips.

Kennedi found an admirer to dance with. Or rather, he found her. He could not have been a day over 10 years old. His smile boasted uneven adult teeth that were shifting their way into predestined places. They held hands and danced together, it was so cute.

His mom, who looked to be more our age, was so smitten. At first, she tried to deter her son from walking over. It was obvious that he wanted to come, he just swayed his young self over to Kennedi. Beaming from ear to ear, she grabbed his hand and they danced together. It was so cute.

"Uhh ohh, Sade is breaking it down, y'all!" I teased. She has no rhythm and she knows it. She was cute though, especially rocking that short, pixie cut.

"You see me! Don't hate," she remarked bobbing her head up and down off beat. She tried her best to find it, it just escaped her. We all have that one friend who can't dance to save their life. An older woman walked over to her laughing and clapping. It was all in fun, they had a good time.

"That's right, Boo! Shake what ya mama gave ya," British encouraged. Sade wobbled harder, even more off beat. We were all laughing at her. It was at that moment, I realized what a bond we had. There were so many years between us; our friendship had grown stronger and stronger. We had all been through so much.

When shit hits the fan, you see who your true friends are especially if you are going through it publically. These days it's hard to find genuine people. Everybody is out for what they can get, a leg up or get some tea. We don't down each other, we don't compete with each other, it's about Girl Power and having each other's backs! Right then, at that very second, we were in letting loose in paradise.

We had to practically drag Paris away from the stand. She was mad that we wanted to keep it moving. She stammered over to the taxi, taking more steps than required. Moving without really going anywhere. It was time to go. We took the yacht out to sea and just jammed out. The captain kept us in somewhat shallow water, so we felt comfortable getting out of the boat and playing around in the water. There is something about the motion of the ocean that seems to take cares away.

The boat was loaded with plenty of snacks to keep us from starving. And yes! We kept the drinks flowing. Even Kennedi finally got her ass in the water.

"Ok, girls! Princess Kennedi is about to get in the water," she began a disclaimer. "No dousing me with water. Ok, chicas?"

She put her precious hair up in a bun at the top of her head and the captain put a lifesaver in the water for her to lounge in. She effortlessly bobbed up and down in the water, the current making love to the air.

Of course you know we had to get her ass. *SPLASH!* Paris's drunk ass swam underneath her and pushed her butt up while Sade pulled the lifesaver from under her. She came up screaming, then joined right in with the horseplay.

"Y'all, this is the last night here," Sade started.

"We're gonna miss this shit for real," British added. "But I'll be glad to get back to my man!"

"You mean Kenya's man," I said. She knew it was coming.

"Why the fuck do you always come...for...me? Did I come for you?"

"British, you can do better. That nigga..."

"Ladies! Ladies!" Kennedi yelled splashing us both. "C'mon now!"

British angrily swam to the ladder and climbed onto the boat. The mood was kinda screwed by that point. The sun had begun making its way to the western part of the sky, we got out of the water and let the yacht take us back to our island, Virgin Gorda. The Divas all made their way to their own rooms to shower and freshen up for a nice dinner. Paris and Madison were talking in Paris' room.

"Why do you think Lola keeps getting on British?" Paris started.

"I guess that's her damn soap box, girl."

"She needs to leave that shit alone."

"Well, when you see someone you love making a mistake, don't you tell them?"

"Yes, the first time and the second time. British has gone back to Stacks more times than a dog goes to the same spot in the yard to pee!" They laughed. "At some point, you'd think British would get the hint."

"One could only hope. Lola probably feels like if she keeps jokingly throwing it out there, British will get the hint."

"Hmmm...I can see that. Lola isn't joking anymore though," Paris shook her head in agreement.

"Lola is right. That situation is definitely not the business. At every turn, Stacks shows her his heart belongs to someone else."

"Just like Trey showed me. Sometimes, you just don't want to read the writing on the wall." Paris spoke in a kinda monotone voice. Madison looked over at her; she could feel it coming.

"That Trey shit was something totally different, Paris."

"It's all fucked up, right? We are pulling for these men to get it right. Men we love who don't love us the same." Paris started to cry. Her eyes welled up easily. "I love him, Madison. I still do. That shit doesn't just go away because somebody fucks you over. Like, what happened to my lover and my friend? Why didn't he just tell me he was gay from the jump? We could have been great friends." Madison walked over to where Paris was sitting on the bed to console her. Madison's eyes welled up with tears, too. All of a sudden, the door popped open.

"What are y'all heffas..." British came in loud and wrong. Madison started shaking her head and the tears fell from her eyes. British looked at Paris who, by that time, was laying in Madison's lap. British came to get me, Sade and Kennedi.

"I'm just so…so…so embarrassed! Did he not think about how this was going to affect me? Did he think about Amarii?" Paris cried. "Y'all don't have a clue what this feels like. This…this hurt and betrayal. This shit is on a whole different level!"

"You're right. I thought my situation was jacked up. It has nothing on this," Kennedi said.

"I have to look in the faces of so many people who knew! I never thought I would lose my husband to another man." I gave her a few tissues to wipe her face and blow her nose.

"Paris," I started, "you can compete with another woman, but you can*not* compete with another man. What Trey wants, you can't give him. You have to just pray for strength to deal with this and wish Trey the best. At the end of the day, you two still have a child together."

"Eye roll emoji bitch! Five times!" British blasted, "Wish Trey the best? Hell no! Fuck that! You should have set his ass on fire with the mattress!" They all laughed. "Oh shit, is it safe to say? Is it too soon? If he was gay, he should have just been true to himself and be proud about it." Sade's stomach growled loudly, they roared with laughter.

"Now, girl you know we are not about to end our trip letting you cry your eyes out on this bed. C'mon now. Let's go eat," Kennedi said.

"Look at my face," Paris said fearful, "I know it's all red."

"Chile, its dark. Ain't nobody checking for you. They're all looking for me," Sade joked and she was the first one out of the door.

We went to a restaurant with prime real estate right on the water. We literally had to take our shoes off to get there. It was so nice. We requested the table furthest away from the restaurant which was closest to the water. As we caught the last rays of the sun dripping down into the horizon, the waiter brought a light to grace the table. It was in the shape of a cone that changed colors against the white table cloth and white chair covers.

"Everything on this menu looks so good!" Sade started. Remember, I told you, her ass is greedy! Even though she was probably the smallest, her appetite was definitely the biggest. You know skinny people can eat!

"You would say that with the tape worm you have in you!" British chimed in, "I don't know if I want crab cakes or fish."

"Ya cyan't go wrong wit eider uh dem," the waiter walked up quietly. We didn't even know he was there. He told us the specials of the day and we collectively placed our orders. We got a round of tropical drinks, the kind that taste good and sneak up on ya.

Since we could catch the free wifi from a neighboring hotel, everybody leapt on their phones. We were all acting like crack addicts, posting pics of us partying in the ocean to Instagram and Facebook, taking advantage of the hot commodity.

The truth is, as a society, we have become so dependent on social media, that for many of us, it's the first thing we do when we wake up and the last thing we do before going to sleep.

Forget praying and jumping up to pee. A choice between the three can seem like a life decision. People jump on social media as soon as that alarm jolts them from their sleep. It's like the world will stop turning if we don't see what was posted while we were sleeping. Logging on for quick bursts, turns into long stints, getting high on 'likes'. Being on vacation is even worse. Yeah sure, it feels great to disconnect, but it also feels like a part of you is missing.

"Ok, everybody...phones away!" Madison said, clapping her hands abruptly. She appreciated the break possibly the most out of all of us. Her schedule was the most hectic. Even without kids. "This is our last night here, let's just enjoy this a little while longer before we plug back into reality."

"It has been crazy not logging on in days," British admitted.

"You mean every hour on the hour!" Paris said.

"Ugh! Y'all always coming for me, dang!"

"It's too easy, British."

"My phone is off!" I said. *Click.*

"That's because you don't even have followers. It's easy for you," British said.

"I do! I have like 200 followers!"

"Lola! Take your page off private."

"I don't want people all up in my business," I said.

"You don't have no business," British blasted. We all chuckled.

"Paris, you aight over there?" British asked. Paris was doing a lot of grinning, not much talking.

"I'm just enjoying listening to y'all argue like little school girls."

"You seem distracted."

"You know," Paris started, "I'm still messed up in the head. Finding out your husband is gay just *does* something to you. From the beginning, this nasty muthafucka was doing who knows what with men...then coming home to me! Why did he pick me? Why did he use me to be his beard? I don't know if I'll ever be able to love again. To trust a man, you know?" The tears coursed down her cheeks.

There was a loud silence as each of us imagined different circumstances where we found out our men were having sex with another man; the kind of thoughts that crash around in your head causing your heart to stop and beads of sweat almost to appear.

"I can't imagine," Madison broke the quiet. "Me and Robert have our issues, and no offense, your situation is just a disaster."

"I mean..." Paris wiped the snot away from her nose, "he never gave me the option. He never mentioned it. Not that I would have stayed if he had. But, he never told me! I just feel so...so...fucked up! Now how am I supposed to move forward like that shit didn't happen? I just keep asking myself why I didn't make a bigger effort when he started changing."

"It's not you, girl!" British shouted unconvincingly. "There is nothing wrong with you. He prefers to be with men. So, unless you are going to grow a penis, there ain't much you can do." British's comedy club stab bombed.

"Even if you had made a bigger effort, the outcome would have been the same, Paris. It just would have happened sooner," Madison said gently.

"I feel like I can't trust guys anymore. How can I believe anything a man says to me?"

"Nope! You can't do that!" Kennedi climbed into the convo. "You can't take past demons into a new relationship. You have to give your next man a clean slate or it'll never work. I know I opened up Pandora's box having threesomes with Ty, which probably encouraged him to cheat on me. But I'm not going to think *every* man will cheat on me."

"They all cheat!" British said matter-of-factly.

"Yeah, with hoes like you around who don't mind being side chicks, it's easy for them to cheat, British." That was certainly a point of contention for British and Kennedi. Kennedi really felt some kind of way about British sleeping with a married man, now that she lost her husband to a side chick. Now British's claws were so deep into a married man that she was imagining a real future with that bum.

"Kennedi is right, Paris," Madison put her six-figure law degree to use instantly putting out the fire between Kennedi and British. "You have to give the new guy a fair shake. Don't drag these drama-filled, sad emotions into new possibilities. You'll only create issues that don't even exist and drive him away."

"Like I did with Doc," Sade added. "I drove my man away. You can bet your sweet ass it won't happen with the next one."

The waiter walked over to the table holding two plates. Behind him was another waiter carrying a round tray with the other dishes. They sat our respective plates in front of us. I peered onto Sade's plate, because she was sitting next to me and there was a big pair of googly eyes staring back at me.

"That lobster is big enough to eat you, Sade!" I said.

"Not if I eat him first," she cracked a claw and dunked it in melted butter.

"Paris, when the right guy comes along, you will know it. You will want to open your heart to him. Sade, you need to not be so driven by money and glam. There are more important things than only having your bills paid. If you cared about the way Doc treated you, you would have kept your damn legs closed," I let them know. Sade cut her eyes at me, I pretended not to see.

"It's definitely too late for coulda, woulda, shoulda's!" Madison threw in, "Sade knows how to handle her situation going forward."

"I'm sure she does, after beating herself up enough about it. Madison, we have to get creative with ways for Robert to bring in that cake," I laughed.

"Well, I didn't ask...but since you seem to have all the answers...what do you suggest?"

"Definitely something other than music. Maybe try encouraging him to really dig into his hobby."

"That's really thinking outside the box, Lola," Madison responded sarcastically.

"British, why are you holding on to Stacks so hard? Do you think he is really going to leave his wife for you? Or do you just enjoy torturing yourself with the twisted fantasy? You are the only one at this table who is putting themselves through a bad situation. Wherever that man is right now, I'm sure he's not thinking about you. I really hope after this trip, you will realize your worth."

"Bitch." British's response was more how she said what she said. Her eyes didn't even blink while she stared at me. She called me out of my name in anger.

"Here we go," Kennedi murmured at the same time as Paris fumbled a fork onto her plate with a loud, *CLUNK*!

"I've just been sitting here listening to you; I respect what you're saying. We all come to you with our problems, giving you all the tea and I feel like you're very judgmental when your shit ain't all the way straight. We come to you because you are the most stable, the most calm and you got your shit together. We look at you like you have the perfect relationship. That may be the case now, but nobody at this table judged you when you had an abortion from being out here hoeing around and didn't know who the daddy was."

That was a real, clutch-my-pearls moment! I think I stopped breathing. As a matter of fact, I know I did. None of the girls knew. Except British. It was one of those moments where you have a secret that you don't want *everybody* to know, yet you still feel comfortable confiding in at least one person. Well, she was my one. And for her to release that devastated me.

"Lola, is that true?" Kennedi asked in disbelief.

"When the fuck was this? I'm so lost right now!" Sade added.

"What's your angle, British? Oh, now you're coming for me?"

"At the end of the day, we are all friends. But you are getting on my nerves singling us out one by one giving us your unsolicited opinion."

"I am *happily* married."

"Lola, get off your damn high horse. I know you ain't coming at me with this shit. Miss My Husband Is A Regular Dude And That Bores Me."

"I am committed to KP," I defended.

"Lola," British snapped her fingers, "quit faking the funk, Boo. Living out here in these shadows almost got you fucked up!" She jumped down my throat. My appetite was being carried out to sea with the waves. Further and further away.

"You're being ridiculous! This isn't about me."

"Why not?" British jerked her head up from her plate. She took another bite of her coconut shrimp. "You always have so much to say about our lives and what we are doing wrong, but the mirror you look at yourself with was so shattered that you couldn't see the problems you created for yourself."

"That's the past."

"And for us, this is *now*. Let us figure out a way to navigate through our own shit so it will eventually be in the past. Please and thank you."

Compared to my friends, I was the 'normal' one, the plain Jane. I had a regular boring job although my husband's was a little more exciting. When I met KP in college, we had high aspirations for our future. We were excited at the prospect of graduating, getting good jobs, and starting a family. Things didn't work out for us right away. We dated a little bit, but at 20, I was not trying to be tied down so the real dates turned into me telling him to swing by my place and bring rubbers.

He was down with it, then things dwindled away. I was having so much fun, I barely noticed I was seeing less and less of him, until I saw him walking around the mall with LaKesha Grant ol' knock-kneed ass. She had a cute face, with that short, 'juices and berries' hair. She was tiny, like five foot even. I confronted KP about it and told him I wasn't crunk about him seeing her. He let me know he was tired of me treating him like an option. That was it, boom, kaput, over! The next time I saw them, they were hugged up sucking face as if their lives depended on it.

I busied myself with studies and clubbing. One of the beauties of going to school in a collegiate town like Tallahassee was the whole town revolves around collegiate-aged people. There was something to do every night of the week. I would see KP around.

Seeing one another had the same effect on both of us. We would look, do a double take, try not to smile, burst into a Kool-Aid grin, then get a little hot and bothered in our pants. He even did it when he was with LaKesha Grant; he diverted her attention rather than let her see what really had his mind occupied.

Somehow, some way, I graduated...Thank you Lordy! Not ready to join to ranks of real adulthood, I went straight through to get my masters in accounting. My friends were living fabulously. They were getting their hair and nails done every week. Between all of them, they were getting the hottest bags and dope shoes from the season's most sought after collections.

I wanted to be the first to rock something for a change. I wanted to see something expensive and hot and own it just by merely mentioning it to a guy with pockets deep enough to splurge on me. I wanted the new cars with upgrades every two or three years.

Taking a trip to Atlanta, I ran into KP. It was almost magical. I was at a club with some friends and wouldn't you know it, as soon as I walked in, he was standing right at the door! I saw him before he saw me. My heart completely stopped beating. I scanned the area real quick, looking for the skank who stole my man, that heffa wasn't anywhere around.

I walked over to stand about 10 or so feet away from him. Out of his reach, but clearly on his visible radar. It was the first time I'd seen him in two years, at least four since we stopped sexing. I stood with my legs spread somewhat apart and stared him in the eyes. Letting the beat take control, my head fell back, I closed my eyes and gyrated slowly to the music. I squinted to see if he was watching, he was. It was so dark in there, he couldn't tell I was squinting.

One of his friends started walking over to me. I rubbed my hands around my neck like they were supporting my head. KP pushed his friend out of the way, walked over and kissed me. We've been together ever since. He was good marriage material, the kind that you dream about when you envision your future.

KP was the man I saw an actual future with. He was ready to settle down and be a one woman man. In our mid-20's, we were still young with the world at our fingertips. We got married a year and a half later in a grand ceremony at the Hilton. Daddy footed the bill.

Before our marriage license was even approved by the State of Georgia, I was pregnant. Guess I got pregnant on my honeymoon or shortly thereafter. We were scared, but excited. My parents were overjoyed to become grandparents. I came from a good home. Both parents in the home, and they are still married, 44 years all in. They did a damn good job raising me and my brother.

When we found out we were expecting twins, there was more pressure. Most of it would be on me since KP had such a crazy schedule finishing school and getting his hours in. My parents jumped in to help, making the process seamless. My boys were born healthy and perfect. Identical.

I was happy to come home from my accounting job to the family I loved so much. KP graduated and started his rounds into plastic surgery. Choosing that specialty of medicine, his hours were set. He wasn't up at 2:00 in the morning like emergency room doctors. By the time he got home, homework was done and dinner was cooking. And…that was it. That was our life.

KP was bringing home that gwap and he paid all the bills. I kept my whole paycheck and went to work faithfully every day. I worked to keep me sane, because staying in the house with twin babies was definitely a kamikaze mission for me.

Most people would be happy to have that kind of money coming in. To me it wasn't enough. I wanted more. You would think I would have been happy to have a husband who was gainfully employed and who cared about me. If I had a bad day, he brought home Nestle Crunch bars or big, sour pickles…my favorite snacks. He sent me sweet texts during the day. He spent time with the boys, but always put me first. He was kinda on the square side. I trusted him completely.

I lived vicariously through the drama and romance of my friends. Listening to those girls was way better than watching a movie. They were living life and having fun. Somewhere between becoming a wife and a mother within nine months, I lost who Lola was.

KP and I were stuck in a rut, a boring routine of work, home, homework, football or soccer depending on the season, showers, bedtime stories, bi-weekly sex and a fierce Atlanta commute. And depending on whether the kids were sick, teething or couldn't get to sleep, the sex may or may not happen. That was where we were.

I knew he loved me and he showed me. I never pumped my gas, he made sure to always fill my tank. I never even had to tell him I was getting low. He routinely "surprised" me with beautiful flowers every two weeks. We went out to dinner for our date nights twice a month. He was incredibly supportive when I applied for new jobs or started working on more certifications.

It just wasn't enough, it never was. I was bored at home and bored at work. Being an accountant is terribly dull. The same thing every day. A cubicle, spreadsheets and stupid meetings where they regurgitated the same info week after week. Where was the excitement? Where was the sense of spontaneity? Why couldn't I fuck my husband in the car in the parking lot when we left our date night? Why wouldn't KP sit me on the island and eat me out like I was his breakfast? Why couldn't he surprise me with a Chanel bag just because he was walking in the mall and liked the color? When was he going to plan a trip for us and tell me in just enough time to pack and scramble to the airport?

One day, British invited me to a basketball game with her. I hated to go on a school night, but I made sure everything was set out for the boys the next day. By that point, they were going on eight or nine years old, so they knew what time it was and how to get themselves in bed. All Daddy had to do was give them the word.

I dolled up in ripped jeans and a cute shirt with some decent pumps. British scooped me up and we went to the game. She was seeing one of the players so we had good seats. After the game, we went to an after party. So, whatever team wins usually has a party to celebrate. Nothing crazy and over the top, but alcohol sometimes drugs, lots of food and drinks.

Going to the party seemed like a good idea. Until we got there and British was all boo'ed up in the corner with her guy which left me alone with no one to talk to.

"Ya girl ditched you, huh?" A male voice said to me. He was standing over me. With me in heels, he was still easily a foot taller than me. Sitting down, he made me feel like a child.

"How did you guess?"

"You look like a lost puppy," he laughed. "Marcus."

"Lola."

"Whatever Lola wants…Lola gets," he started singing.

"That's why my mom named me Lola. She loved that song."

He walked around the bench and sat down. For the next hour or so, we talked. I kept glancing in the corner to see what British's fast ass was up to. They went from standing across from each other, kissing, to his hand up her skirt. All I could do was shake my head. But sitting there, it all became clear to me why she and Sade craved being in those types of environments.

It was so electrifying to be surrounded by money. Real money. Ballers. Tall, muscular athletic types who could buy you just about whatever you wanted. They made sure you ate good and fixed your drinks. It was fast and fun and free. It was the kind of place that makes you forget about your problems in the real world.

When British was finally ready to leave, I introduced her to Marcus. I thanked him for keeping me company and walked out. He followed me out of the party and asked for my number. I was hesitant, but I gave him my work number.

Marcus was my dude. I was sure he had other chicks, but they didn't matter to me. When he was with me, he made me feel like the only girl in the world. He gave me that fresh relationship kinda feeling, all giddy when I saw him or when he called.

It was exciting to steal away for a few hours and meet him in a room, have wild crazy, I can't get enough of you sex, then go back to my normal life. It made me feel attractive, wanted, something KP wasn't giving me anymore. Marcus had popularity and money, especially groupies…yet, he wanted me. Little ol' me. I got caught up in it, I couldn't show him that though.

Marcus told me the reason he fucked with me is because he could tell I wasn't the same as the washed-up, cookie cutter, plastic girls they see in every city. I had a real career and something going for myself. He

never interfered with my married life. I never interfered with whatever he had going on.

He was younger than me, by about six or seven
years. And, oh, did he have a sex drive. Seeing him for
a few hours here and there wasn't enough for me. I
wanted more. I craved him. We talked on the phone
every...single...day...I started feeling the need to
spend some real quality time with him.

I told KP about some bogus conference that I
made up with my job and took a few personal days
from work so I could travel on the road with him. We
had been seeing each other for a whole year by that
point and were very comfortable. He had to squeeze
me in where he could. It was basically four days of
Marcus and I, nothing else. KP was able to handle
getting the boys to school and had his assistant pick
them up from after school.

Selfishly, I was no longer imprisoned in my
boring routine of a life. I was able to get the release I
deserved, just not in the way that a wife and mother
should. Whenever I was sad, Marcus sent me money.
If I had a bad day at work, he sent me money. He
bought me a pair of Louboutins that I lied and told KP
I splurged on because I just had to have them. KP
wasn't that tight on my wallet so I could buy things
like that every now and then. Marcus bought me a few
bags as time went on. We had a long talk about him
pumping the brakes on the gifts. I was still married and
had to be able to explain everything.

The incident British was talking about came
after about two years in. I found out I was pregnant.

Obviously, I didn't know who the father was. By that point, Marcus rented a condo in Atlanta during the off-season so we could see each other more regularly. There was absolutely no way to tell who the father was. He said, he didn't know why I was telling him. I mean, why would he get a condo to be near me just to have that attitude about being with me?

I was crushed. I didn't expect him to be overjoyed, but I did expect him to care. I had no plans on keeping the baby. I couldn't. Sitting in the clinic waiting room, I got in my damn feelings. I felt like for the length of time I had been giving him some of this sweet stuff, he would have been singing a more supportive tune. He wasn't and it drove me absolutely insane.

Seeing Marcus' reaction scared me straight. I literally wrote down a list in my head of pro's and con's comparing my husband to my boyfriend. There was no comparison. How was I going to rob my sons of the very family life I grew up in and was proud of? I couldn't bear the thought of looking in KP's face telling him I had been having an affair. Much less that I had gotten pregnant. He had not done anything to deserve the way I was treating him.

My hubs was so in love with me and it was evident. We all pray for a man who stays at home chillin', who is respectful and will take care of home. When that man arrives, we dissect him, look for flaws, get bored, and don't appreciate him. Nah, we are into disrespectful type dudes, the guys who keep our attention because we are so busy trying to keep up with their every triflin' move.

I had an abortion. That was my turning point. Sitting in the waiting room looking around at the other chicks about to endure the same fate, I wondered how I had gotten there. The truth was, I was married to a man who practically kissed my feet, but sprung on a man who probably wouldn't notice if I never called him again. My husband worked hard to provide a good life for me.

I prayed that God would deliver me from the guilt I felt. I knew there was a tough decision to make. How would I have been able to explain to KP that the baby may have been someone else's? How would he have reacted? I couldn't crush the man like that.

I cut Marcus off. It was hard…and I ran back a few times. Our whole dynamic had changed. I saw him through different eyes. I thanked God for my husband and my life. I promised I would never end up in that situation again.

Instead of going out looking for excitement, I created it. Whatever spark I felt I needed, I had to ignite. I started speaking my husband's love language again. Just like he made love to me by taking care of me and the boys, making sure the bills were paid and making the house a home, I had to do the same.

I made love to him by being faithful, letting him know I had his back and finding new things and new places for us to experience together. It was up to me to ask how his day was and be interested enough to listen.

My boys were looking at their mother as a model for who they would find in a wife.

"Lola, I know you are trying to get your life together and be the perfect wife *now*, but you have skeletons in your closet just like we all do. Just because you got past your issues doesn't mean you can look down on us because our problems are not in our past...quite yet. We are figuring it all out just like you did. You did some fucked up shit in your past too," British took that moment to really go off. She had the whole head rolling, neck popping, finger waving thang going on.

"Yes, I fantasize about being with Stacks, because he gives me the feeling it *looks* like you have when you are with KP."

"Do you realize what you have in KP?" Madison interrogated me. "He cooks, he cleans, he cheers you up at the drop of a dime, he buys you just because gifts. He pays you attention, chick."

"I have to harass Stacks for a fraction of the attention your man gives you," British tagged on to the direction Madison was headed.

"Ty only seemed to give me negative attention," Kennedi sang. Her voice sounded like a sad love song. "This man will do anything for you, Lola. Anything! I wouldn't mind living a normal, life if I'm comfortable and catered to!"

"KP possesses the qualities all of us are looking for in a man. You have him and you're taking him for granted. How do you think that makes us feel?"

Finally, I had to interject. They were jumping on me. If I was big enough to dish it out, I should have been big enough to take it. What I wanted to say was... I never wanted to think about that day at the clinic again when I shared my darkest secret with this bitch who told everybody at the table. Instead, what came out was...

"If it seems like I'm being judgmental and hard on you girls, please understand that it's coming from a good place. I'm only saying this because I *love* my divas for real! Look, I've been through some shit and could have easily lost my man. I had to ask myself if I was doing my part to keep my home happy. Seeing y'all out having fun and trying to be like y'all chasing the type of men British and Sade were running behind, I lost sight of realizing I already got something solid. And I know he loves me unconditionally. He kisses the ground I walk on!"

"When I was cheating I didn't get that same love, but I would push my hubs off like, ugh, he's a square, he's lame. Not even thinking he was the same man I prayed and asked God for. Looking at your situations shows me how *not* to lose a husband. My friends out here looking crazy because they looking for industry guys with money and those dudes don't always have the respect for you. Money can't buy love and class or teach him how to really be a man. He can only buy you things to keep you happy for the moment. Is he listening to you? Does he really care how your day was? I have all that in this man and I almost lost him. I want y'all to have y'all shit together and be with someone who really loves you. Not be somebody's side bitch. We are too old to be sneaking around in dark corners to fuck somebody. Don't let a man just run your life to the point where you lose who you are."

"Yes, that happened five years ago which is why I am the way I am now. I'm not saying I'm perfect by any means, but I try to help my friends save their relationships and be more respectful of themselves. I made fucked up decisions and mistakes in my life and I want better for y'all, I'm not saying I'm perfect. Just know if I'm seeing some shit that's fucked up, I'mma call you out! Because I love you!" I was crying by the time I finished. I really meant every word I said.

"Let's make a toast," Kennedi said. "Here's to real friends who are like family...who you actually like more than family. Here's to sistas who have your back no matter how bad things get, no matter how fucked up you are, sistas who accept you for who you are. Here's to happiness and making dreams happen."

"Cheers!"